WHAT COULD POSSIBLY GO WRONG?

Copyright © Mark Sedon 2022

www.kiwiskiguide.com

First published 2022

All rights reserved

No part of this book may be reproduced or transmitted in any form or by any means, electronic or mechanical, including photocopying, recording or by any information storage and retrieval system, without prior permission in writing from the publisher.

A catalogue record for this book is available from the National Library of New Zealand.

Soft cover ISBN 978-0-473-59290-5

Edited by Geoff Walker

Design & layout www.yourbooks.co.nz

Printed in New Zealand by www.yourbooks.co.nz

This book has been printed using sustainably managed stock.

WHAT COULD POSSIBLY GO WRONG?

[signature]

MARK SEDON

Never waste a day

CONTENTS

Introduction 1

PART ONE - Growing Up

1	Growing Up	7
2	The Party Years	13
3	Saving Lives	19
4	Venturing into Mountaineering	26
5	A Proud First Ski Descent	30
6	Fiordland and a Proposal	36
7	Big Wall Climbing	41
8	Becoming a Guide	47
9	Venturing Overseas	55
10	Skiing the Peaks	58
11	Skiing in a War Zone	64
12	Completing the Seven Summits	67

PART TWO - Escaping Catastrophe

13	An Avalanche that Should Have Ended It All	75
14	A Volcano Erupts	88
15	A Fatal Helicopter Crash	94
16	Is My Brain Exploding?	123
17	Blowing Stuff Up	132
18	Mount Everest	142
19	Starved and Trapped	167
20	Thrills in the Southern Ocean	180
21	Falling, Falling	187
22	To the End of the Earth	193
23	Now and into the Future	215

INTRODUCTION

It's amazing how fast life can change. From enjoying the time of your life, to almost losing it. A split second, a small mistake, a shift in events can kill you, cause an injury; or you might just sneak through, unknowingly escaping catastrophe by the smallest of margins . . .

I've had a number of such events (well, the ones that I've known about), such as breaking my back when I was buried in an avalanche, watching helplessly high up on an erupting volcano, almost dying in a catastrophic helicopter crash, a severe brain haemorrhage, dropping a burning sack of explosives onto a helicopter skid, a 10m fall into a crevasse, starving for five days in a shipping container in remote Papua, and a yacht fire and broken mast in the Southern Ocean.

I've seen accidents happen to others — a Sherpa high in the Himalayas whom I saved as he was about to fall out of his harness, a friend being swept away by an avalanche, and a 200kg pulk (sled) dragging a mate backwards into a crevasse . . .

What could possibly go wrong? is a phrase I have stopped saying aloud.

I've written this book to share some of the unbelievable survival stories that I've been involved in. You might think of me as unlucky to have had so many near-death experiences. But I think of myself as extremely lucky to have got away with them. I am most definitely a 'glass half full' sort of person.

I have a saying: 'I am very afraid of dying, but I am even more afraid of not living.'

I don't think the things I do are crazy, or excessively risky. All the things I do I have trained for, rehearsed, slowly got better at over time and planned as thoroughly as I can to minimise the risk. I have the right gear and, critically, wait for the right weather. I go with suitably experienced friends and we support each other. But I accept there is risk in what I do. But then I am sometimes more fearful driving at 100km p/h just one metre away from someone I don't know coming towards me doing the same thing than I am of stepping out of a helicopter with my skis on a 1-metre-wide mountain top with steep snow-covered slopes below me. Perceived risk is very relative to where you are standing and what your background is.

There is a saying printed out and stuck to the wall of my office right next to my computer that says 'Life's journey is not to arrive at the grave safely in a well-preserved body, but rather to skid in sideways, totally worn out, shouting MAN what a ride.'

The feeling skiing gives you is hard to explain to a non-skier. A non-skier might ask: why would you risk the danger of an avalanche? Let me try and explain. Snow is made up of 75-95% air, 5 to 25% water. Skiing on 30 or 90cm of fresh cold powder snow is a feeling very difficult to explain in words. The feeling of weightlessness, of floating on an imaginary bed of the silkiest soft down imaginable. The feeling gravity gives you as you accelerate down the mountain with the soft snow gently pushing back, slowing your descent. The feeling of effortless movement, the euphoria, the sheer joy it brings to my soul is immeasurable and unforgettable. Sharing it with friends and clients creates a feeling of ecstasy and happiness. It's not adrenaline filled, more a sense of calm satisfaction. It is a feeling I will chase until the end of my days!

Introduction

I've divided this book into two parts. The first part covers some of my varied outdoor adventures in different places around the world. The second part, which I've called 'Escaping Catastrophe', describes a series of events in which spectacular things really did happen and my life was often seriously in danger.

What could possibly go wrong? Well, sometimes it does! Happy reading.

Part One

Growing Up

1

GROWING UP

I was born in Burwood Hospital in Christchurch on 12 September 1969 to an 18-year-old mother (Jan) and 21-year-old father (Fraser). After my brother Jonathan (Jon) was born they saved enough money and took off on their OE, with a four-year-old and a one-year-old. They bought a camper van and travelled around Europe for a year, working at odd jobs to make ends meet.

In New Zealand a typical holiday for us was to take off from Christchurch to places like Quinney's Bush or Woodend, to camp and spend time in the outdoors. At about the age of 10 during the school holidays I flew to the North Island where I had uncles and aunts living on large farms. They owned and/or managed large sheep farms and I was the gate opener. I was given a box of .22 ammunition and sent to shoot birds roosting above the clothes lines, or to hunt possums and rabbits. I loved the freedom to roam with a gun and a motorbike.

In 1982, when I was 12, we uprooted and moved to Auckland. Our parents were tired of Christchurch's wind; it was either the north-easterly or the north-westerly and it had been driving them nuts. We settled on the North Shore and with Mum and Dad both working long hours they got ahead and bought a 28-ft launch, *La Tortuga* (the *Turtle*), which had a top speed of just 5 knots. She was an old wooden boat with just enough room to sleep four, with an outdoor shower, a kitchen and an upstairs bridge. The interest rate for a second mortgage in 1985 was around 23% and *La Tortuga* was bought entirely on mortgage. We'd load our food and fuel and, with the pontoon almost touching the water, motor out of the moorings for two to three weeks at a time. We'd explore the Hauraki Gulf, Great Barrier Island, and the Mercury and Kawau Islands. We caught plenty of fish and I also passed my basic PADI scuba diving licence, so I was able to gather scallops and crayfish, mostly diving alone, which of course was never ideal. Looking back, I see that as young boys Jon and I were starting to accept more risks than others — and quite comfortably too.

After our parents separated, we sold the boat and I took my scuba gear to Browns Bay, where I swam out alone to look for scallops in the murky city waters. I'd blindly grope the sea floor with my bare hands and sometimes find a scallop, sometimes an old shoe or other rubbish.

I remember coming home from Rangitoto College when I was 13 or 14 to a truck delivering every kid's fantasy — a year's supply of Cadbury Caramello chocolate. There were 156 king-size blocks, all with the same delicious flavour. It turned out that Dad had entered a creative writing competition to describe how the caramel gets inside the chocolate. It was something he'd never done before, and he won first prize. We ate the year's supply in three months! It seems amazing that Jon and I, who are now in our 50s, still have very few, if any, fillings.

I wasn't a natural sportsperson. I was useless at rugby and had given that up before leaving Christchurch. I wasn't fast enough to be a back and didn't like the idea of wedging my head tightly between two guys' hips in the forwards. More importantly, I couldn't catch the ball well enough. I was better at cricket, but only through sheer determination and a lot of practice. We played for hours and hours after school every summer's day. Mum would never let us turn on the TV after school and we were sent outside to play with our mates. I was a bowler and not great at batting, although I made it into the second XI at school before I discovered skiing.

Basketball was my winter sport and we played this for hours and hours using the hoop at our neighbour's house. We invented a game where if you missed, your mate got to punch you on the arm; this provided excellent motivation to improve. Unfortunately my neighbour Paul was a basketball rep, so he usually beat me. I often had a bruised arm.

I was lucky to get through my teenage years in Auckland without a criminal conviction, serious injury or death. I was drinking and driving – and I was an idiot. On my 15th birthday I sat my driver's licence test and failed but passed on the re-sit a couple of weeks later. I'd driven too fast during the practical. From then on Friday and Saturday nights entailed buying beer and driving around the North Shore looking for parties. We often ran out of fuel and after midnight we'd revert to syphoning petrol from parked cars. Looking back, it was really bad form. I was lucky I found skiing, which diverted my energy to a more constructive activity.

On one particular night we syphoned enough petrol to fill our tank then poured several litres onto the road, set it on fire and took off down the street. Behind us a wall of flames stretched across the road. The road was a dead end, but we only realised that after taking off at high speed in the wrong direction. I turned the car around and sped through the wall of flame with fuel spilling out of our uncapped tank. Then I had to stop in a hurry so my friend could vomit out of the car door – he'd taken one suck too many on the syphoning hose and had swallowed petrol.

Shoplifting was another School Certificate studying technique. I'd met Andrew, a friend from another school, while I was away on our boat. He wasn't much into school and we'd roam the Takapuna shops, lifting whatever we could. One day when there was a tent display in the mall, we blatantly walked up to it, selected a suitable tent, packed it away and walked off with it. No one questioned us or looked twice. We were well-dressed schoolboys in uniform with an innocent-looking appearance, so we probably didn't look like typical thieves.

This habit ended abruptly with a visit to the police station accompanied by my parents. My brother's friend, who had lifted some of the stolen goods from my bedroom, had been caught by his parents. Luckily the decent people we'd stolen from didn't press charges and we got off with a stern warning. My partner in crime, Andrew, wasn't so remorseful and quickly reverted to his old ways, while I distanced myself and discovered skiing on Mt Ruapehu in the centre of the North Island.

I was 15 when our neighbours took me to Mt Ruapehu to try skiing, and I absolutely loved it. I wasn't a natural and on the first day I was so afraid that I couldn't go up the first chair, despite my friend Paul's encouragement. With perseverance I ended up getting a taste for it and started working at the local Foodtown supermarket packing groceries, to save to buy a car and to support future trips to the snow. I moved up the ranks at the supermarket from being a checkout operator to a storeman, so I could afford my own skiing equipment. I wagged school regularly with my friends and drove down to Mt Ruapehu for long weekends. It must have been obvious where we'd been when we came back after a 'sick day' with raccoon-style suntanned faces.

About this time, I won a day trip which may have also set me on the right track. I was selling lottery tickets for a school fundraiser and after walking the streets for days I ended up selling the most tickets. My reward was a trip on the yacht *Lion New Zealand* skippered by Sir Peter Blake. He'd recently won his fourth Whitbread Round the World Race. I was spellbound by this weathered-looking guy who had made a career out of his passion.

Fireworks time was always exciting and when I look back, it was great training for avalanche control in years to come. Double Happys were every boy's favourite if you lived in the 1980s. Long before they were banned, those bangers obliterated fruit, models, sandpits and more as boys embraced the sheer joy of blowing shit up.

We'd poke Double Happys in mandarins, light them and throw them at each other across the street in play fights. We also held small freshly-lit skyrockets in our hands and shot them at each other. Sometimes we'd drain all the gunpowder out of crackers and fill a letterbox with it, then blow it up (not ours). Unfortunately one day this happened to be on the walk to school. The upset owner called the school to complain and I got dragged out of class.

The dean informed me I'd committed a caning offence and marched me into the boys' toilets, along with another teacher as a witness. I bent over and touched my toes as he lashed me twice, with as much force as he could muster, with a metre-long bamboo cane. Sitting on my chair in the classroom that afternoon was painfully uncomfortable. That night I showed the two 50mm-wide welts to my horrified mother. She was shocked, but my father said I deserved them. He was right, I probably did. Needless to say, it dampened my appetite for blowing up letterboxes.

My first memorable adventure was with my shoplifting mate Andrew on Great Barrier Island, 90km off the coast of Auckland. We were 14-year-old high-schoolers. We'd been dropped off with ancient external-frame packs at Tryphena Harbour on the southern end of Great Barrier by our parents in their boats. I had a 2kg stereo cassette player hanging round my neck that was blasting Talking Heads, and we were full of enthusiasm for the adventure ahead. The idea was to trek north to Port Fitzroy and rendezvous there with our parents.

We set off along an unsealed road with feeble teenage shoulders. But when we realised how much we hated trekking, we decided to hitchhike. The first car to stop was an old taxi and we paid for a ride to a campsite.

During my later years at school I skied in New Zealand at every opportunity I came across, including road trips to the South Island. I even tried one run of heli-skiing at Mt Hutt in 1989. But I couldn't ski the powder and struggled down the run. The trips always included scams such as forging letters from our old school stating that we were still students, so we could get student lift prices. I had a friend who was 21, and this meant we could rent a camper van. We'd park it outside the pub in Methven so that we'd never have far to go home after drinking ourselves silly. I sometimes wonder if we remembered to remove the student ski passes from our ski clothes when we visited the pub – most likely not.

I'm sure many teenagers have trouble deciding what to choose for a career when they are 16 or 17. It seems so important then. I wanted to be a pilot in the air force and my maths marks were good enough, but in my sixth-form exam results I was bottom of the class for English and not much better for physics. Those were the other two subjects I needed to pass before I could apply, so I went back in the seventh form to redo both subjects. That didn't last long when I found out seventh formers were not required to attend class. So I was never going to pass because I spent hours and hours avoiding any study while I played cards with my skiing friends and planned future skiing trips. Usually we played '500', using subtle sign language to tell each other what cards we had. We easily beat everyone we played against.

My other strong subject (I only had two) was technical drawing. It was then that I decided to become an architectural draughtsman. I knocked on a few doors and found a job, quit school and enrolled at polytechnic to study part-time towards a degree.

2

THE PARTY YEARS

For the next three years I worked diligently (after finding a new job after my first employer went bankrupt) and saved money for an overseas ski trip. I took on a second job working nights in a bar. I wanted to go to Canada for the winter and be a ski bum. In my free time I watched reruns of ski movies such as *Blizzard of Aahhh's*, and the New Zealand classic *The Leading Edge* and any ski action I could find. One time I rented a movie from a video shop (this was pre-internet), used two VHS players to copy it, then removed the screws on the video cassette and swapped the insides so that I'd have the original before taking the copy back to the shop.

Most Kiwis are encouraged to travel when they are young and I was no exception. But I wanted to travel and ski. My sights were set on Banff, a well-known resort town in Canada. I placed an advert in a Banff newspaper asking if anyone had a house to rent and was surprised when I received a letter offering me and my two friends a three-bedroom apartment close to town. This was a rarity. Houses were in short supply at that particular time. Who in their right mind would offer theirs to three 21-year-olds?

We set off for Canada late in 1990 just after my 21st birthday. We bought a car in Vancouver and drove all night through a howling blizzard over the Rockies and arrived in Banff at dawn on the coldest winter in years. There was a six-week period when the daytime temperature didn't rise above -20°C and it dropped to -35-40°C for several days.

Banff was a busy little ski town in those days, surrounded by tall pine trees and even taller rocky mountains with piles of snow several metres high along the sides of the roads. Elk roamed the streets, and everything was bear proof, from the garbage bins to the house waste. There were three local ski resorts – Mount Norquay, Sunshine Village and Lake Louise – and we bought season passes to ski all three.

We had a few brushes with the law while in Canada. My friend John didn't seem to catch on very quickly that being intoxicated in public was an arrestable offence and spent many nights in the local police station's cells. His final classic fail was driving home well over the legal limit when he attempted a U-turn only to mistime it and drive up onto the footpath where he knocked down a bus stop sign, right in front of a waiting police car. Mine was to come later in the winter within an avalanche enclosure . . .

It was before Canada and New Zealand had the work-visa exchange, so I worked illegally as a dishwasher in a Swiss restaurant while during the day I skied. I completed an instructor's course and with skiing around a hundred consecutive days my skiing improved dramatically. It didn't matter how much we drank at night; we'd always manage to ski every day.

In 1991 Kiwis could obtain a one-year working visa if they arrived in the UK with £1000. So after the winter in Canada I landed at Heathrow on the final leg of my one-way ticket with £10 to my name. When the customs officer asked me how much money I had, I confidently said £1100 and hoped he wouldn't ask to see it. He simply stamped my passport with my work visa and said welcome to England. The bluff had paid off, now I just needed a job. Ten pounds was just enough to catch a train to Bedford, where Penny, John's girlfriend, lived. Later that day I had a job as a bartender in the local pub.

It was quiet in Bedford so a week later I moved to London and found a job managing a bar in the Norfolk Hotel in South Kingston. I found England dark and dreary, and, sadly, I socialised with very few English people. London was full of Kiwis, Aussies and South Africans but, like nowadays, I always wanted to meet local people when I was a visitor in another country. I went to the usual tourist spots and tried to stay fit for skiing by rollerblading to work through Hyde Park. That was, on its own, quite dangerous. Several times I'd be out of control and needing to tackle a lamp post to stop myself from sliding in front of traffic at inte sections.

My focus was on working and saving money for my next winter of skiing – this time in Austria. It wasn't easy. I might have been living in London, but I was earning a bar wage and spending much of it on beer, chasing girls and partying. I decided to go to St Anton in Austria and get a job for the winter. I bought a train ticket via Holland, Germany, Bulgaria, Czechoslovakia and then on to Austria. I intended to live cheaply off a loaf of bread and a jar of jam for my three meals a day.

I was staying at a backpackers' lodge in Prague, which had a bar and a beautiful bar girl. Czechoslovakia had not long been open to foreigners and the bar girl was into me. We spent the evening chatting and flirting while I drank. I was sure it was a mutual attraction and wasted no time inviting her to my room, which to my surprise she accepted.

It was late and as no one else was around she started closing up the bar. Her father was the owner and just as I was about to leave, he walked in behind her as she was leaning over the bar chatting to me. He caught my eye and lifted a large foot-long knife to his throat, making an unmistakable slicing motion. The lovely girl didn't even notice the shock and panic in my eyes as I quietly excused myself and went to bed, locking the door behind me. She didn't talk to me the next morning before I checked out quickly and headed for Austria.

I spent a couple of weeks in St Anton unsuccessfully job hunting and more successfully getting drunk most nights. Needless to say, my money ran out quickly. I had enough for two or three more days, so on a whim I hitched a ride to Ischgl, another ski town about an hour away, and went door knocking. At the first hotel I was offered a job straightaway with a room, three meals a day, a ski pass and over a thousand dollars a week working shifts morning and night washing dishes. My afternoons would be free for skiing. It was perfect, but even so Austria could have killed me.

I shared a room with another Kiwi called Chris, and I was working for a bunch of good-fun Austrian chefs in a four-star hotel. They took much delight in getting us to test their homemade glühwein and then going out with us and partying the night away. We'd all be back at work early in the morning and after the shift they'd all go home for a sleep while I went skiing. At 5pm we'd be back in the kitchen working the night shift before more glühwein 'testing' and another night out. I'm not sure how we found the energy.

After winter in Europe, I went home to Mt Ruapehu for the New Zealand winter because my friends had been writing to say the snow was really good. I started out for home via Greece and Egypt and a trip up the Red Sea to Jordan, where I got a special permit to travel through the West Bank to Israel.

I loaded up the white van with five other tourists whom I didn't know and quietly left Amman, the capital city of Jordan, at dawn. It had taken me three days to get a permit to travel through the highly militarised zone. We arrived at a short narrow bridge on the border of the West Bank where sandbags were stacked up at each end and troops were lined up pointing sub-machine guns at each other. Needless to say, things looked a bit tense. The Jordanian army checked our passports and permits, then dragged the wire barrier aside and our nervous-looking driver drove slowly onto the bridge between the two opposing sides. We stopped in the middle of the bridge and four Israeli soldiers, who looked like actors in a Rambo movie, slowly approached the van with their guns pointing at us.

They looked in the front and then checked the passports and permits before sliding the side door open, guns pointing through the door at me in the back seat. The soldier examined my passport and broke into a wide grin.

'Ah, Kiwi,' he said and lowered his gun. Then the guy behind me showed his US passport. The soldier grunted, raised his gun again and pulled the guy roughly out of the van. After going over his paperwork, looking through his gear and questioning him, they allowed the American back into the van and we drove through the Israeli barrier and off the bridge.

That night we partied in Jerusalem, laughing about the experience. Dancing at a night club with beautiful female Israeli soldiers wearing army gear and carrying sub-machine guns. Pretty wild for a Kiwi.

Back in New Zealand I bought a season ski pass at Mt Ruapehu and signed up for the unemployment benefit (the dole). Mt Ruapehu (2797m) is one of New Zealand's most active volcanoes and forms the highest peak in the North Island. It has two ski areas – Turoa and Whakapapa. My friends John and his brother Jamie had rented a house that had a spare room for me. The dole was $150 a week, rent was $26, firewood was scavenged, and by living off two-minute noodles, old discarded food from the mountain cafés and porridge I had enough money left at the end of the week to get drunk.

Our old railway house was just 10m from the main trunk railway line. At first I'd wake up with a fright during the night as the house shook and my room was lit up by the train headlights as it rumbled past.

I went on to spend a decade working and playing on Mt Ruapehu. I got to know the mountain's moods and temperament well. It's a fascinating mountain, extreme in so many ways. When the weather is bad, it's really bad, and when it's good, it's amazing, with views over lush rainforest to the ocean and other snow-covered volcanoes.

It was the winter of 1992 when I first met Jo Cunningham, whom I would later marry. She was the mâitre d' at the restaurant where I worked part-time. My first impression of her wasn't a good one – I didn't like her. I wanted to have fun and she was too bossy. I remember one night when I knew I'd be late for work because I'd drunk too much. I thoughtfully slept in the restaurant on the bench seat. I woke in consternation with Jo pouring water in my ear to wake me up. Guests had started arriving for breakfast, and were no doubt amused. At that time Jo lived with her partner and I had no interest in her at all, until . . .

After the winter I headed back to Austria to wash dishes, ski and save enough money to complete a five-day medical course and a seven-day avalanche course (around $3000), which were the prerequisites for applying for a job on the ski patrol.

3

SAVING LIVES

Back on Mt Ruapehu, armed with my avalanche knowledge, I made my first voyages into ski mountaineering. I'd hike up to the icy summit, or the Girdlestone Peak, alone at first then dragging others, and ski the backcountry. I remember climbing the Girdlestone when it was so icy that I had to drive the tails of my skis into the ice, move my feet up then repeatedly kick the toes on my ski boots into the ice to get a 2cm notch to step up, then move the skis up. Looking down between my legs at 300m of steep 50° ice, I didn't feel that secure and thought I should probably invest in the crampons I'd seen others use.

Later that winter of 1993, armed with the avalanche qualification and pre-hospital emergency care course, I convinced the ski patrol director to let me work as a volunteer. Two weeks later someone resigned so I was offered a full-time paid job. It was the start of a decade of mountain rescue. I loved the bad weather; the worse it was the more I delighted in it. It taught me many, many mountain survival skills including avalanche training and loads of challenging medical practice.

We often undertook cliff-rescue training which was a fantastic way to learn from other more experienced guys. I really enjoyed that, and I received great instruction in general mountaineering techniques while I was at it. I learnt from books also and practised a lot on real-life rescues. Turoa was carnage in those days with five or more medical helicopter evacuations every weekend. I learnt how to relocate shoulders and kneecaps, give intramuscular injections, suture, and look after severe head and back injuries – all in a mountain environment. I also carried out cliff rescues on ice as difficult as any rescue in the Southern Alps or the Himalayas.

With so many people around, it was the perfect spot for a young ski patroller to learn some skills. I remember one particular day when the mountain was closed because of terrible weather – gale-force winds and heavy rain. We had to stay on the mountain as medical backup for the maintenance staff while they de-iced the lifts and fixed storm damage. Those guys were tough, walking around the mountain in overalls and carrying a 'yeti stick'. This looks like a baseball bat and is used to beat rime ice off the lifts. Rime ice is super-cooled water droplets that freeze when they collide with a structure or a rock face on a mountain.

The maintenance crew were inside having lunch when I went to take our daily observations at the weather plot. Rugged up in wet-weather gear, goggles, climbing crampons and carrying an ice axe, I walked around the side of the building. The noise of the wind was like a freight train. As I walked out past the end of the building the wind hit me like a sledgehammer, blowing me sideways and off my feet.

I slid several metres along the icy surface trying to self-arrest using my ice axe, a technique used for stopping a fall down a mountain, to prevent being blown across a flat slope. It worked. I ended up near the weather plot. I crawled over to it and carried out the observations. To return to the safety of the ski patrol hut I had to front-point into the wind, with my belly on the icy snow, swinging my ice axe in above my head. Again, a method used for climbing steep ice, not to get across a flat ski slope. An hour later I struggled into the safety of the building, much to the surprise of the other members of the ski patrol who hadn't realised I'd gone outside.

Eventually we had to leave and ski down to the base area. The maintenance crew had walked down. Skiing down under the Giant Chairlift I noticed something I'd only ever heard about but never actually seen. In one specific area the wind was so strong, combined with certain slope characteristics underneath, that it forced the 150kg three-seater chair to be repeatedly blown up and over the cable in a helicopter-style fashion. The beating these lifts took during each storm really tested their design to limits unlike those faced by any other ski resort in the world. We noted down the chair number, and when the storm cleared the maintenance crew took off the chair and checked it over while allowing the steel cable to untwist.

When radio calls are received by the ski patrol, you never quite know what you'll be responding to. Always ready and trained to deal with the worst possible injury, more often than not we'd face an RTD, or an AFK (ski patrol terms for Ruptured Tear Duct or Another Fuckin Knee). But Turoa in those days (1993-98) and Whakapapa (1999-2000) were sites of complete pandemonium, especially at weekends. The hard snow conditions combined with a clientele that lived mostly on or near the coast, in sub-tropical New Zealand, with very limited mountain awareness, often created multiple accidents.

We set off up the mountain early, before the lifts had opened, erected slow signs and fences, checked that the grooming was okay and made sure the ski lifts were all running properly. Everything needed to be ready for the 9am opening. Then it'd be back to the ski patrol hut, where we'd put sandwiches or pies scavenged from the cafeteria the day before into the toasted sandwich machine. Then we'd wait. We knew it'd come. Ten ski patrollers, all trained to various levels of medical and technical rescue, waiting and chatting, or skiing if the snow was good. There was usually somewhere great if you knew the mountain as well as we did.

Then like clockwork the calls would start to come in. We'd respond with a rescue sled in tow, skiing fast and confidently through the skiers and snowboarders to the accident site. The patient would be assessed and if it was something the first responder could handle alone, they would load the patient into the toboggan and ski with him or her to the clinic. It'd take an hour or so to take them down, assist the doctors in evaluation and treatment, then return up the mountain with the toboggan, ready for the next call.

It wasn't unusual to have two to three accidents a day that were life or limb threatening, or serious enough to need helicopter evacuation. Many of us enjoyed the sort of accidents that would challenge and excite us. It sounds a little sick, but I think it was the adrenaline. As long as I didn't know the patient, I found it easy enough to deal with most unsightly injuries. There were a few times when I knew the patient and that was much harder to deal with.

I remember responding to what sounded like a serious accident in an area called the Amphitheatre. As I skied into the bowl, I spotted a streak of blood running from a rock down to a man below who was not moving. Game on! I called for immediate backup as I kept skiing at speed towards him. 'Bring oxygen, breathing equipment and a backboard,' I called over the radio. We always taught site and self-safety and I told two men to stand guard high above to make sure no one fell on us. I snapped out of my skis and knelt down to grab the patient's shoulder and ask if he was okay. I knew he wasn't, but that's what you do when you approach an injured person.

He responded by blowing bubbles through blood in his mouth. His scalp was peeled open from just behind his forehead to the back of his head and I could see a tennis ball shaped compression fracture in his skull. He was breathing slowly and there wasn't much else I could do until backup arrived. I put him on oxygen, fitted a neck collar and with help rolled him onto a backboard – no easy task as he weighed over 120kg.

Once he was in the toboggan I skied it out of the icy bowl with another ski patroller holding tightly onto a tail rope to stop the toboggan sliding sideways down the slope. It wasn't easy, and if we'd slipped we would all have fallen a long way onto more rocks. We kept an eye on his breathing while we skied to the base area where the doctors were waiting. He was flown out shortly afterwards and after a long convalescence he recovered just fine. He even came back to thank me, which had never happened before and was very cool.

Another memorable rescue was responding to a report of a group of people stuck on a clifftop high in the ski area. I skied over to the location and as I got closer I realised it was a large group of people. An entire family of Indians, dressed in their city clothes – right down to their dress shoes – were clinging to a rock. I had no idea how they got there unscathed, over the slippery ice, about 2km from the top of the scenic chairlift ride. All they could do was smile and with a small sideways head wobble say what a beautiful day it was. I couldn't argue. We fixed a rope and cut some steps and an hour or two later they were safely riding the chairlift down to head home to Auckland with a great tale of survival.

There were also embarrassing moments as a ski patroller, like falling over under the lift. Because you were dressed in red, it was hard to escape a cheer and a laugh from the people riding the lift. Or riding around the ball wheel of the lift after the toboggan or your pack straps had got caught on the chair, preventing you from dismounting. I remember one very funny call when a patient being transported by Chris had fallen out of the toboggan. We were all amused, and Chris had to buy the beers that night.

On one occasion I escaped unscathed and unseen when I was transporting a knee-injury patient in a toboggan. I hit a patch of super-hard ice and the toboggan spun around below me. I was looking uphill and going backwards. I kept the turn going and completed the 360° spin, somewhat surprised that I was still upright. The patient yelled out, asking if everything was okay. Fortunately he couldn't see much because the tarps were protecting his head from the flying snow.

'Everything's fine,' I replied. I'm fairly sure he couldn't hear the shakiness in my voice.

When a storm hits, it not only deposits several metres of snow on Mt Ruapehu, which rises above a beech forest just a few kilometres from the moisture-soaked winds of the Tasman Sea, it also deposits the infamous rime ice that grows on everything – buildings, rocks, lift towers and lift cables.

The workers on Mt Ruapehu are never far from their trusty yeti sticks. I remember seeing the chairs on a chairlift touching the ground between the towers, encrusted in several tons of rime ice and dramatically stretching the steel lift cable. One hit from a yeti stick can cause all the ice to dislodge from the chair, but this can also cause the chairs and the cable to slingshot up so forcefully it can launch the cable off the tower. When you whack the ice with all your force at other times, just a small dinner-plate-sized chunk will fall off.

The de-icing crew risked head injuries, losing fingers and toes, lightning strikes, wind, rain and ice. But those guys loved it and I enjoyed helping when I could. It was on one of those days that I met a torpedo.

I was up a lift tower on the Moro T-bar, which is no longer there. It was before safety harnesses and helmets were compulsory, so once I was comfortable 8m up the tower, it was time to strike the dramatically sagging cable, encrusted in a 30-40cm diameter cocoon of rime ice. Sometimes the ice is brittle and the entire 80-100m length of ice can fall off with one hit, ejecting the cable upwards, while at other times only a chunk falls off. On this particular day about half a metre fell off. Your whole body vibrates when you hit the ice; it hurts your teeth, your elbows and your back.

I hit it again, directly on the cable this time where the ice had fallen off. Another metre fell off. Bugger! Then I studied that entire section of ice. There was 80-100m between me and the next tower. Then the ice uphill started sliding down the cable, turning slowly because of the twisted cable underneath it. I hit the cable again and 2m fell off, but the mass of ice on the cable started moving faster and turning faster. I hit it several times and every time a few metres fell off, which was good, but the remaining ice on the cable picked up more and more speed and spun like a torpedo, making an increasing whizzing sound. It was exciting and nerve-racking as I swung with all my might, as fast as I could.

Eventually I knew I was losing the battle; the ice was moving at high speed towards me from above and spinning loudly. There was nothing I could do but turn and grab the lift tower and cover my head. The torpedo smashed into the lift tower wheels, large chunks of ice, which were hard as rock, exploding all around me. I escaped with a few bruises. Luckily the force of the ice that hit my tower had also dislodged the ice from the cable below. The lift tower swayed violently with the force of all the ice falling off and I held on tight until it stopped. Then I climbed down and skied down to the next tower still with ice on it.

After a winter in Canada and two in Austria, I had built up debt with my parents. It's hard to earn enough money to party, ski every day and travel the world as a ski bum. It was then that I took a job in Japan during the 1993-94 winter as a lift operator, hoping to move on to ski patrolling. I worked days for the first time in five winters and skied at night under lights on my days off.

After working there for the winter, I was able to pay off all my debts and buy some climbing gear, and I even had enough left over for a deposit on a $30,000 piece of land in Ohakune.

4

VENTURING INTO MOUNTAINEERING

Totally excited about my new mountaineering equipment, which I bought after the winter in Japan, I wasted no time skiing to the top of the frozen waterfall at Turoa, where I set up a rope to climb it. I buried my skis as an anchor, clipped my rope in and put on my crampons. The two main rules with crampons are: never stand on your rope with the sharp points and always walk with your legs far enough apart so that you don't hook your pants with your sharp-pointed crampons.

I clipped into the rope, then stumbled when my crampons caught on my new climbing pants. I'd ripped a big hole, which caused me to trip onto my new climbing rope. But things improved after that. Together with my friend Kane I climbed several first ascents on Mt Ruapehu's frozen waterfalls, on one occasion actually placing our first-ever ice screws while leading a first ascent on vertical water ice. Not easy, but it was a way of learning I adopted, jumping in headfirst, giving it a go, despite taking on way more than my skills should have permitted.

Somehow I ended up kissing Jo at a party in the Hot Lava nightclub. She was looking stunning and we were both drunk. She led me outside and kissed me. I was very surprised, but not one to argue.

I was a full-time member of the ski patrol in 1994 and I think part of the attraction for Jo was being able to jump the lift queues. She'd wait near the back and I'd come past calling out for a single.

One day Gordie, one of my fellow patrollers, was de-icing some rimed trail markers on a ski piste. These signs were mounted on 2cm-square steel poles to survive the severe icing. After each storm we'd need to beat them with our wooden yeti sticks, then with a power drill insert a new hole in the snow to deposit the trail marker. Gordie was happily at his work when a skier came flying down at high speed and crashed into him. Both went flying and lost their skis and gear. Gordie was uninjured, but the skier had smashed his face in. He was bleeding and had teeth missing. Gordie called for backup to help package the seriously injured skier and shipped him off to see the doctors at the clinic.

In those days our doctors were two young, attractive identical twins from South Africa, Liesel and Celeste. When you wheeled in a patient, with or without a head injury, and the girls looked over the patient from each side, the look on their faces was always amusing. So Gordie left his patient there, a little cross with him for taking him out. He picked up his yeti stick and while riding up the chairlift, noticed two of the patient's teeth imbedded in the end of it.

Mt Ruapehu was entrenched with tales of survival and medical drama. There was the tale of the groomer driver working late at night on his own. When he started the lift to ride up to his groomer, the lift stopped halfway up for no apparent reason. He was without a radio and it was before the days of cell phones. Therefore he had two choices: spend the night on the chair, which he might survive, or take off all of his clothes, tie them together to make a rope and lower himself down, hand over hand, to the ground. This is what he chose to do. Then he ran semi-naked to the base of the lift, started it and ran it until the chair he'd been stuck on returned to the base with his clothes attached.

Broker than Broke

In November 1996 Jo and I went to Snowbasin Ski Resort in Utah. I had a work visa through the ski patrol exchange programme and Jo was able to work as a snowboard instructor.

The day we arrived, with almost no money to our names, we borrowed a friend's car to drive to the ski resort so Jo could have a look around (it had yet to open). I was assured that the car had insurance and off we went. Obviously driving on the right side of the road took some concentration, but we managed to reach the car park just fine. We looked around then headed off down the mountain road. Unfortunately my concentration had slipped, and Jo was engrossed in our maps. I pulled out of the car park on the wrong side of the road and I had just driven around a corner when a car came towards us. I slammed on the brakes. The other driver did the same and we almost avoided a collision as we weren't going very fast – but not quite. We hit each other, our car sustaining the most damage. I was feeling pretty bad about damaging the car and I offered to pay the insurance excess. That was when I found out the car was uninsured and I was liable to pay for the entire car. We were already so broke; it took months of work to pay for it.

When Jo turned 30 on New Year's Day in 1996, there was still no snow. I'd been given work getting the resort ready for opening, but then we found out there was no more work and no more money. We were so out of pocket that I resorted to 'borrowing' a birthday candle for Jo's cake from the local supermarket. After the small celebration, I put the candle back in its wrapper and took it back to the supermarket.

The snow came and with it lots of work and we eventually

paid off the car. All things considered, it ended up being quite an enjoyable winter.

When winter was over, we took a road trip with our friends Brent and GR to Red Rocks near Las Vegas. We camped in the desert with the glow of the city lights in the distance. The night sky was so surreal I couldn't stop staring at it. We climbed our first multi-pitch rock route, reaching the summit late at night. We were without torches and had some difficulty descending in the dark. Jo was well and truly thrown in at the deep end, having never done free-hanging abseils before, let alone three of them in the dark.

We headed back to New Zealand for the winter.

5

A PROUD FIRST SKI DESCENT

Winter couldn't come fast enough. I was now senior enough to start work early setting up the mountain and checking all the gear. I still aspired to take up more ski mountaineering, so I took a week off work so Kane and I could drive south to see if we could make the first ski descent of a peak called Mt D'Archiac (2875m). We'd spotted it from the head of the Tasman Glacier.

We'd heard there was a farmer in the area with a small helicopter and we hoped he would fly us into the mountain. We tracked him down and paid him cash for the flight in. It was most likely near the end of the time when you could pay a farmer to fly you in, without him worrying about liability. Back then you looked after yourself and didn't blame someone else for your misadventures.

The doors had to be removed so the three of us could squeeze into the only seat in the Robinson helicopter. Our gear, in an old sack, was hanging underneath and spinning slowly as we flew up the Havelock River. I could see the sack under us quite easily as half my body was sticking out of the door. The helicopter was used on the 70,000-acre Mesopotamia Station and not designed or powerful enough to land at the altitude we wanted – about 1500m.

We turned and headed up the Forbes River, the machine working hard because our weight was at the limit. It was then that the farmer said he couldn't land safely on the Forbes Glacier. We flew just above the glacier and he dropped our skis, climbing and camping gear. They sank into over a metre of soft, fresh snow.

The helicopter was still not light enough to land, so he dropped Kane below the glacier then flew back up with the intention of dropping me by our gear. Even then he didn't think he could land safely, so he flew slowly over our gear, a couple of metres above the snow and told me to jump. He wasn't joking, so I climbed onto the skid and when I thought the snow looked okay, I let myself slip off the skids and fall into the snow.

Thankfully I sank up to my waist in fresh snow. He flew back and picked up Kane and did the same thing before he landed next to us and we threw the sack in the back. With a wry smile and a wink, he was gone. We were left there, with our hearts still racing from the ride, up to our waists in fresh snow, two days' walk from civilisation with Mt D'Archiac towering above us. Yeeha!

First things first – we needed somewhere to sleep. We headed up the glacier towards Separation Col. Once we were there, we chose a snow cave site and the digging began. Two hours later, we had a comfortable place to live in. Two beds, a table and a chimney. This was to be home for the following three nights.

4.30am came very quickly. Porridge was cooked and eaten in a hurry, and we were off. It was eerie skiing over to the base of our route on the eastern edge of the south face in the darkness. By the time we got there, light was seeping into the mountains. We lashed our skis to our packs and roped up. Climbing through waist-deep cold powder snow was not a fun way to start the day. Once we crossed the bergschrund the slope grew steeper.

The steeper the slope, the shallower the snow. Soon the slope angle reached 50-55°. That meant perfect climbing conditions, but we had underestimated the steepness. As the hours went by and we looked down, our intended ski route was looking more and more unlikely. We came upon 5-10cm of freshly snow-covered hard ice and as we climbed up the face our route headed out above massive cliffs. The higher we climbed the bigger they got. There would be no room for the slightest slip – if we decided to ski it.

By midday we were on the low peak on a beautifully clear but very cold day. We both agreed there was too much risk involved in skiing the route we had just come up. One mistake, even just a minor slip, would probably be fatal.

Keen to keep moving and stay warm, we struck out for the summit, from where we would search for an easier descent. The summit ridge was exposed and very sharp. It dropped away for several hundred metres on either side and at one point the ridge was so pointed I had to sit with one leg on each side, straddling it. In order to move I had to dig my ice axe into the snow in front of me and pull my body towards it. Snow blew into my glasses and I could barely see anything. The skis on my back kept catching the wind and threatening to push me off the ridge. After 30m the ridge widened out and I set up a belay to bring Kane across.

The wind dropped off as we climbed the final few metres to the summit. The view was spectacular – the West Coast, Aoraki/Mt Cook, and the numerous glaciated peaks of the Southern Alps. It was so amazing that we ended up sitting near the summit for over an hour.

With the time approaching 2pm we thought we'd better start moving. We were both excited about skiing down and the north face looked promising, although quite steep. With adrenaline surging through our blood, we stepped into our skis and got ready to go. I skied carefully down from the summit, on a narrow ridge about 50-55°. On my left it dropped away for several hundred metres over cliffs; on my right it was steeper than the ridge and I couldn't see more than 20m in front as it dropped away out of sight. It was jump turn, sidestep a little, followed by another ever so careful jump turn.

The snow was running down in front of me, dropping out of sight. What if there was a cliff below us? I thought.

'What could possibly go wrong?' I said to Kane over my shoulder.

Sidestep a little, jump turn, stop, sidestep, jump turn, stop.

Every turn had to be perfect. I worked my way slowly down for a couple of hundred metres and stopped in a safe spot. Now it was Kane's turn. He did the same, skiing carefully to where I was. The snow was wet from the day's sun and the avalanche danger was high. We skied down a little further and the steepness relented a little. We stuck to small ridges to avoid the chance of being swept away by an avalanche.

By then we could see much of the terrain below us, which was a continuous 50-55° slope, leading straight into a large open bergschrund about 600m below. Kane skied onto the slope and stopped dead. It was ice! We hadn't realised the time and the sun had gone off the slope, allowing it to freeze solid. He inched his way back, ever so cautiously, until he was safely on the ridge.

'What now?' he asked.

Neither of us were keen on risking a big slide, so we pulled out the rope and dug a snow bollard. This is when you dig a tear-shaped trench in the snow and loop your rope around it. We clipped into the rope, still with our skis on, and abseiled down the icy face. After four 25m abseils we were on less steep terrain.

The rope went back into the pack and we were off again. With legs burning from holding on with every toenail at every turn, we eventually made it to Revelation Col. The intense stress of 'no-mistake' skiing was over. We could relax. There were no longer large ice cliffs, bergschrunds and long icy slopes looming below us. We were so stoked; we had made the first ever ski descent of Mt D'Archiac.

I hadn't met Alistair before. But after a couple of phone calls we'd arranged for him and his South American llamas to travel up the Godley Valley to meet us after our climb. After five days in the mountains I was hoping our rendezvous would eventuate.

I was pretty happy to see Alistair and his three llamas coming up the valley towards us early the next day. The introductions were followed by careful repacking of our gear into packs specially designed for the llamas.

I ran ahead to take photos and laughed to myself at the sight of the llama train walking down the riverbed with our skis and gear strapped across their backs. It was a sight normally only seen in South America, not in a New Zealand mountain valley.

We arrived at Tekapo and after a large burger with fries washed down with a cold beer, we spread out our bed rolls under the trees next to the road and slept well.

The next day we hitched back to our car and headed north to Ohakune for the winter.

Jo and I spent three months in the summer of 1997-98 travelling the South Island, living in our tent and car and doing as much rock climbing as possible. It was a summer filled with adventure, new friends and living cheaply. Jo was on the unemployment benefit and I was selling photos and stories. We survived off very little money indeed. I was also working on a book idea – a table-top photography book on New Zealand rock climbing.

To aid our financial misery, just before we set off we bought an old house and moved it onto my land in Ohakune. It was a three-bedroom villa that we'd spotted on drums an hour south of town with a 'For sale' sign on it. We made an offer, then borrowed the money from the bank, adding a little to renovate it with. Unbeknown to the bank we used some of the mortgage to make our payments for the summer while we travelled around the South Island.

We arrived in Wanaka in January 1998. There's a climbing spot called Roadside and we were climbing a route called Shortcut to Exposure when a guy arrived, turned on his car stereo and blasted us with funky dance music. He and his friend set about climbing several hard routes in quick succession while we bumbled our way up the easiest route at the crag. We arrived back down at the same time. There was barely an ounce of fat on his body and his smile was broad.

'My name's Dave Hiddleston,' he said. He was a mountain guide and a local legend, having established many of the climbing routes. Little did I know he'd become one of my closest friends and my mentor for mountain guiding. We chatted for 30 minutes and by the end of the conversation he'd offered us his sleep-out to rent and free rein of his house at Lake Hawea while he went away on a guiding trip. Around 25 years later we still live at Lake Hawea, but sadly Dave died in an avalanche on New Year's Eve in 2003.

Dave Hiddleston was a huge inspiration to my outdoor career and personal ambitions. He was the most motivated person I've ever met, and he had a cheeky sense of humour and a wry smile. He was short and well-muscled and an extremely talented athlete with an appetite for adventure and good times. These ranged from climbing Mt Everest to setting dozens of new rock and ice routes in New Zealand, to folklore stories about riding through the dark, wet Homer Tunnel holding onto the roof of a car at high speed while probably not sober.

Dave was killed while guiding on Mt Tasman when a small avalanche swept him, two other guides and three clients off the north shoulder. Only two of the six survived the fall. It was a huge blow to me, Jo and our entire community. Hip had reached and inspired more people in his short life than most will in two lifetimes. He was so talented I just couldn't figure out why he didn't work out there was avalanche danger. I'm sure he wasn't thinking clearly, for whatever reason. Because it was a small avalanche, maybe he just missed it? Hip's death seriously dampened my appetite for undertaking difficult personal mountaineering trips, but I continued to guide.

His friendliness was typical of people in Wanaka. Everyone seemed to be going somewhere or had just come back from someplace. They all seemed to be driven to enjoy life and never waste a day. We loved it and spent some time living in Dave's sleep-out. He also encouraged us to have a go at a route he'd just completed on the north buttress of Mt Sabre in Fiordland. So, armed with his beta (beta is short for information on the climb) and a photo, we went into a remote corner of Fiordland . . .

6

FIORDLAND AND A PROPOSAL

The river roared below my feet as I painstakingly placed one foot in front of the other on the thin three-wired bridge. Normally this crossing would have been a breeze, but I was carrying a heavy pack full of ropes, food, climbing, camera and camping gear. It pulled me from side to side as I made my way across Moraine Creek, 15 minutes into our eight-hour walk to Phil's Bivvy, our base camp, for an attempt on Mt Sabre.

The rich green forest, sometimes clinging to the steep valley walls, featured mostly tall silver and mountain beech trees. Underneath the canopy of beech the terrain was covered with crown ferns, while deep-green spongy mosses and lichens grew on rocks and tree deadfall. There was water everywhere, with patches of bog next to mountain streams, and the air was damp with moisture. The dense native bush shaded us from the hot summer sun as we climbed steeply for three hours. The scenery was outstanding. Spectacular rocky mountaintops peeked at us between breaks in the forest and time went quickly as we plodded along.

The travelling was tough through long grass over uneven

boulders. A twisted ankle was not what we wanted, but it was just what Jo got when she stepped onto an uneven piece of ground. I was unsure of the extent of her injury, and after five hours of walking we were still only halfway – things were looking gloomy. After soaking her ankle in a nearby river for some time we had to decide whether to go on, find shelter for the night or go back.

We decided to go on. Our pace was slower, but we had to make it to Phil's Bivvy because we hadn't brought a tent. The bivvy was a large, overhanging boulder with room for six people to sleep in and stay dry in the worst weather Fiordland could throw at us.

When we finally reached Lake South America, we could see Phil's Bivvy. It looked so far away and it was getting dark, so we settled for Gill's Bivvy, only 200m away. Unfortunately Gill's wasn't so easy to find, but we located it just on dusk, 10 hours after starting out. We ate dinner straightaway before we bedded down in the most comfortable bivvy I've ever been in. Eight beds had been smoothed out, with dried grass to sleep on. The rocky roof overhung the sleeping area by some metres and the ground was warm and dry. Sleep came easily.

It felt as though it was only minutes later when my alarm went off at 6am. In the dark I struggled to check out the weather. We were enveloped in cloud and it was drizzling. Oh well, back to sleep. By 7am the rain had stopped, but Mt Sabre was still surrounded by cloud. Mmmm – more sleep. By 7.30 the cloud seemed to be clearing. We got up in a hurry, ate our porridge, packed our climbing gear and by 8.15 we were on our way.

As we headed across the basin the day was perfect. Not a cloud left in the sky. Jo's ankle was sore, so we hadn't committed ourselves to the climb – yet. My mind was running through the calculations. It was going to be a dark, difficult and dangerous descent. Reality set in and we decided it wasn't worth the extra risk. Decision made, we took a seat and a minute to enjoy the gorgeous face of solid black and silver granite sparkling in the morning sun. What a mountain!

'I wonder what the poor people are doing?' I joked.

Unfortunately we didn't have time to wait for the next day.

So we packed and headed out another way. Gifford's Crack is the more direct, although more technically difficult, access to Mt Sabre. It's a steep gully comprising rock and tussock. 'Stand on the rocks and pull on the tussock,' I instructed Jo.

On reaching the top we were rewarded with some of the most spectacular views in the world – Milford Sound with Mitre Peak standing proud, the glaciers and summit of Mt Tutoko as well as Mt Sabre and numerous other mighty granite peaks in all directions. It was undoubtedly one of the most dramatic views in the world.

It was then that I picked a wild daisy, got down on one knee and nervously asked Jo, 'Would you marry me?'

She freaked out a little as she'd always said she'd never get married or have children. She sometimes jokes that she thought I might leave her there if she said no. So she agreed and we relaxed and enjoyed the moment for a while before heading on to find our way down.

Seven hours after leaving our bivvy rock we were heating our last packet of noodles in a warm hut. We tried Sabre twice more, both times unsuccessfully. For us the peak would remain elusive. We still hear stories of climbers spending a long cold night sitting on the summit having not climbed it quickly enough.

We had a wedding to plan in the spring. Once we were married Jo would also be entitled to a work visa if we went back to Utah. That was the plan.

December 5 1998. Wedding day on the flanks of Mt Ruapehu in the native bush below the snow line. It was a fitting place, the mountain and its people meant so much to us. It is still the only day I've worn a tie in the past 30 years, and it was a special occasion. Jo's mum had died the year before, and her dad a decade before that. It wasn't a big wedding, but it was a lovely occasion. About 50 friends and family gathered in the small clearing with native birds singing all around us. Jo wore a deep blue lace dress that glistened in the sunshine and looked beautiful. Charles, a local Maori elder, sang a karakia and we drank bubbles in the warm spring sunshine. A JP performed the short ceremony and we repeated our vows, signed the marriage licence and headed down to Ohakune to a local restaurant for the evening with dinner and dancing.

Soon after that we headed to Fiji on our honeymoon, then Utah for the winter. The exchange rate on the NZD to USD was almost double, so we were able to earn good money as well as save.

Learning from My Mistakes

When the patrol director position became vacant at Turoa, and because I was the most experienced patroller, I applied, fully expecting that it would be just a formality and that I'd be given the job. Unbeknown to me, a junior patroller friend who was a close friend of the manager also applied and much to my utter disappointment *he* was given the job. I was gutted. But a few weeks into the winter of 1999, Budgee called from Whakapapa Ski Resort on the other side of the mountain and offered me their avalanche forecasting job. I jumped at it because it was an awesome opportunity to run my own snow-safety programme. I craved a more challenging role.

Budgee and I became close friends over the next two years. We hung out together all day, every day. Like me he partied hard and played harder. I had a saying that you should never waste a day off with a hangover, and he certainly didn't. We talked continuously about things we'd both done or wanted to do. Most of his stories centred around sex and women, while mine were more about climbing and skiing.

We were the top dogs of the ski patrol. The day would start with a cooked breakfast in the café while the other patrollers set up the mountain. Once the snow softened, we'd put on our skis and go for a few runs. I was also the avalanche forecaster for the backcountry, and we'd drive a skidoo to the crater and dig profiles or just drink beer.

But when there was avalanche control work to be done, or

accidents to attend, we were diligent. We were like brothers from a different mother, best of mates, laughing at each other's stories, although Budgee had far better ones than I did.

I was desperate to go to Antarctica and the easiest way appeared to be working for Antarctica New Zealand at Scott Base. The best qualification for this was the NZ Mountain Guides Association course. I was more of a skier than a climber, but to qualify for the ski-guide course you had to do an extra pre-course. I chose to do the climbing course first, even though I hadn't done a lot of climbing.

Jo and I moved back to Wanaka that summer (1999) and I climbed as many alpine routes as I could to get experience for my guide's course. I also wrote stories for several magazines and got some extremely good exposure for rock climbing in New Zealand with stories in the world's biggest climbing magazines in America, Australia, UK and France. I also sold the idea of a New Zealand rock climbing photography book to Craig Potton Publishing.

The following winter of 2000, Budgee convinced Whakapapa management to fund my first summer guide's course and be paid while I was on it. Six weeks before the course I went down to Christchurch to train with the other participants and get fit for rock climbing. The guide's courses are tough. If you fail on client safety, you are automatically sent home. Of the six of us on the course, three failed. I passed with good scores; my mountain rescue and avalanche skills crossed over to guiding and my years of taking Jo rock climbing had helped me develop guiding skills.

But I didn't repay Budgee very kindly. After the summer working at Snowbasin in Utah, Gordie offered me the job as the avalanche forecaster for Treble Cone ski patrol in Wanaka. I never went back to Whakapapa.

7

BIG WALL CLIMBING

I was keen to try big wall aid climbing, so after a winter in Utah we headed to Red Rocks in Nevada. Aid is when you place protection in the rock, clip a ladder made of webbing to it, stand on it and reach as high as you can to place another piece. By repeating this process, a climber can climb much more difficult rock than they could ever free climb. Free climbing is regular rock climbing when the protection is only there in case you fall.

Every day on our way to the climb I looked up a steep valley at the intimidating Rainbow Wall, a 500m vertical to overhanging cliff sticking high up out of the desert with its smooth red rock face split by massive cracks and corners, the base of which was 700m above the road. I was eager to try my first big wall.

We'd made a new friend while camping in the desert. Adrian was also interested in climbing his first big wall. We talked, climbed together and talked some more. My heart was racing just at the thought – two days on a wall, sleeping, eating, climbing, living in the vertical world. The decision was made – yes, we would try it.

Our wake-up call at 4am came swiftly. There was actually no

need to set an alarm; I was staring wide-eyed into the darkness when it went off, planning and checking I hadn't forgotten anything. We ate our porridge and hit the road. By 5am we were at the trailhead, dawn just starting to break.

The first test was the huge hike up to the base of the cliff, almost 700m above us. Our packs were heavy, with water for two days adding significantly to their weight. But the early morning temperature helped the hike go swiftly. By 7.30 we were standing at the base of the Rainbow Wall, necks craned, staring up at the route.

Adrian led the first pitch at a pleasing pace, fixed the rope, set up the haul system and started hauling the 'pig'. The pig is the name big wall climbers give to their haul bags, a specially designed tough bag with all our gear in it. It had to be tough because it was dragged up the wall by a rope. I started climbing the rope behind the pig with the aid of mechanical ascenders or jumars.

I organised my gear anxiously for the second pitch. The crack above looked difficult. I managed to place a few of my smallest wires, although they were far from secure. The only option was a skyhook move. A skyhook is a steel hook shaped like a bent finger. It is hooked over small ledges and then carefully, ever so carefully, you stand on it.

I had climbed until my waist was at the skyhook. I was sweating and my heart was racing as if I'd just run a marathon. I pushed half a camming device into a flaring crack high above me then stood with care on the cam and watched the skyhook fall off the small rock edge I'd placed it over. No going back, I thought, and carefully climbed high on my aiders. These are a ladder made of webbing which is clipped to each piece of gear so you can climb up. Standing on tiptoes, while I held my breath, hoping the protection I was hanging from wouldn't pop out, I could just reach a bolt to clip. Whew! After a couple more moves, I made it to the anchors.

The next couple of pitches went smoothly, if not a little sluggishly. By the time one of us had led a pitch, fixed the main rope, hauled up the pig and the second had jumared up the rope, cleaned the gear and then re-organised the gear, almost two hours had passed.

Adrian was leading pitch five when he climbed up over a bulge and disappeared from sight. I was hanging in my harness enjoying the view.

'Shit!' he shouted from above. I looked up. He was falling headfirst past the bulge. Fortunately, the rope held tight and swung him back upright. I yelled up something funny, but his pale face didn't seem to understand the humour of his predicament. In silence he headed back up.

We got to Faith Ledge at 8pm, totally exhausted. We levelled out our sleeping areas and made ourselves as comfortable as possible on the metre-wide ledge. My bed was between the wall and a boulder, with my feet hanging over the edge of the cliff from mid-calf. The lights of Las Vegas were spectacular and we ate our dinner as we delighted in our unreal setting high above the desert. My diet for the two days consisted of bagels. Breakfast was two bagels and a banana; lunch was two bagels with cream cheese and dinner was two bagels with sardines. We were loving the challenges of the climb, the location of the wall and the exposure!

I woke in the morning to the sound of birds chirping, but in a sleepy doze felt myself sliding down my foam pad. My knees were hanging over the cliff. Just before my whole body slipped into the void I came to in a hurry and stopped myself, although I was tied in. What a wake-up call. It was no wonder my first priority for the day was the toilet.

How did I accomplish that? Well, climbers must carry solid waste up the wall with them. So number twos are done into a plastic bag. This is then sealed and put into another plastic bag, then put into a piece of PVC downpipe with screw caps on each end.

I laid my bag carefully on my ledge and lined up for a poo. Then I looked down. I'd missed my bag by 15cm. Thankfully I was dehydrated and could put my hand in the bag and grab the solid waste. Then I hygienically reversed the bag and was able to safely store the contents for the rest of the climb.

The hours passed rapidly and so did the pitches. By 4pm we were on the summit, about 1000m above where we'd started the morning before. Handshakes and wide smiles were exchanged before we relaxed in the sun for a while, drinking the last of our water. The reality that we'd done it gradually set in – the wall rookies had made it to the top.

Later we drove straight to the supermarket and bought beer and ice cream, the two things we'd dreamed about on the way down to keep us going.

Adrian and I parted with a handshake and didn't keep in touch. It was before email and Facebook. Funnily enough, we bumped into each other a decade later in the Himalayas; we'd both become guides and were leading expeditions to the far corners of the planet.

After the following winter in Utah, Jo and I jumped on a Greyhound Bus bound for Yosemite Valley. It dropped us at a remote bus station at 4am. We rolled out our sleeping bags and mats and slept in the street until a local bus came to take us into the valley.

Jo suffered from a terrifying and debilitating fear of heights. She bravely battled through this to complete several long, exposed rock climbs. We climbed the 400m Half Dome, the Royal Arches and several more long, moderate climbs. But she had no intention of going with me to climb El Capitan, the 1000m vertical face that brought fear even to me as I stood below it.

El Capitan is a massive kilometre-high vertical to overhanging wall of perfect granite that provides an arena for world-class climbers to test their skills. The Nose of El Capitan was the first climb completed on the wall way back in 1958. It has since been free climbed by inspirational female climber Lynn Hill in one day. I climbed three times on El Cap; there was one failed attempt on The Nose and a two-day ascent of The Zodiac, then an astounding life-changing five days on a route called The Shield.

For the super-exposed climbs, I had to meet up and rope in strangers I met in camp, especially for a route I'd heard about called the Lost Arrow Spire.

At the top of the climb a rope is stretched tightly across a 100m-high void, where on either side the cliffs dropped a further 900m all the way to the valley floor. It was hailing and snowing at the same time and we'd got totally soaked. I had set up the rope and was about to test it. I checked my buckles and carabiners for the fourth time.

"What could possibly go wrong?" I said to my new friends as I swung out onto the rope. The exposure hit me instantly as I started pulling myself across the rope towards the main cliff, 40m away . . .

I had wanted to experience hard-aid climbing, which is called A4. This is real climbing with dangerous fall potential (20m plus), marginal gear placements and a big scare factor. I met two young, strong Norwegian free climbers who didn't know much about aid climbing and were keen on a big wall. We set off up the 1000m Shield route, one of the most spectacular and steepest lines on El Capitan, with five days' food and water. The first 15 pitches were slabs, which the Norwegians led, while I hauled the gear. This was extremely hard work when the route was under vertical and the bags were being dragged up the rock causing friction.

The next day I led the first aid pitch which climbed out of a 10m-wide roof, high above Yosemite and with huge exposure. A few moves after the lip of the roof I had to complete a free climbing move to reach the anchors, but my legs became tangled in my aiders and got stuck. Eventually my fingers reluctantly released from the rock and I fell backwards, swinging insanely under the roof, 600m up the wall. The exposure was intense. It almost made me vomit. I closed my eyes, sipped water from my Camelbak and pushed aside the panic for a few seconds, then climbed back up and got to the anchors.

That night we camped high on the overhanging headwall on our portaledges with music coming out of a small transistor radio. We were bathed in the last of the pink afternoon sun, with the full moon already rising across the valley. Although I was weary from a tough day of climbing, I was stoked to be in such a wild location. When Pink Floyd's 'Wish You Were Here' came on the radio, that was perfection. More than two decades later that song still reminds me of that evening.

8

BECOMING A GUIDE

Having completed all the courses relevant to ski patrolling; several medical courses, the highest-level avalanche course, and obtained a licence to use explosives via helicopter, avalauncher and hand charging, the next logical step was a ski-guide qualification.

A prerequisite to the course, besides the avalanche and medical courses, was a 10-day mountain skills course. Arrogantly I decided I'd do the climbing guide course first. I say arrogantly because I really hadn't accomplished much mountaineering. Not enough to get on the course. But my years of guiding Jo up long, exposed rock routes, my search and rescue experience and my medical skills all gave me a certain confidence to give it a shot. However, before that I needed to complete more difficult technical climbs around Aoraki/Mt Cook.

In the summer of 1999-2000 Jo and I rented a room in a house in Wanaka. Jo worked as a waitress while I wrote and sold stories to magazines in New Zealand and around the world. I met another wanna-be guide, Simon, and we teamed up to attempt the difficult grade 4 and 5 climbs, which we needed to do to be accepted for the guide's course the following summer. With the climbs done I sent in my application for the guide's course later that year.

Then, after a summer of climbing and writing, we headed back to Ohakune for another winter of work on Mt Ruapehu. By then it had become obvious to Jo and me that the South Island was where we wanted to live and Lake Hawea, near Wanaka, was where we liked it the most.

That spring I passed the course and, armed with the first level of guide qualification, headed back to Wanaka to look for work and wait for our American work visas and another season in Utah. We lived in the campground, or, more accurately, Jo did, while I went on guide work. A guiding company gave me two clients and sent me off up Tititea/Mt Aspiring – something which isn't done these days. Now you are first sent out to work with an experienced guide playing more of a mentorship role.

The trip went well and I enjoyed climbing Tititea. I went on to climb this peak 27 times, all but twice on guide jobs.

In 1996 when Rob Hall had died on Mt Everest, I'd read about Guy Cotter buying his company, Adventure Consultants, from Jan Arnold, Rob's partner, and I'd heard that he was continuing to run high-altitude expeditions. I don't remember why I wanted to climb Everest, or when I first decided I wanted to try, but I wrote to Guy. I told him about my ski patrol skills (avalanche and medical experience) and also my photography skills and said that I'd love to join a trip to climb Mt Everest to help him get publicity. I said I'd work for free in exchange for the trip and he could have all the photos.

I thought it was an excellent deal, but Guy must have thought it was a ridiculous offer. Even so, he took the time to write back explaining diplomatically that I couldn't come for free, although he'd give me a healthy discount to join as a client. I'm not sure if he ever remembered my letter, but years later we became the best of friends and I did work for him as a guide on Mt Everest.

Despite Guy's huge success in the mountains and in business, he has always remained an incredibly humble and down-to-earth person. He is one of the world's most well-known mountain guides. I always enjoy it when someone wanders over, obviously in awe of the person they are about to meet, and he throws out his hand and says, 'Hi, I'm Guy,' then waits for them to introduce themselves. It is a humble and friendly way to say hi, even though there is no real need to say what his own name is. As with Budgee and Hip, he inspired and motivated me in life. We always have fun together, no matter what the job is, from filming British princesses to guiding grumpy billionaires or even just emptying drums of sewage. He is super motivated in life and in business and is probably my most financially successful self-made friend. Although the COVID-19 pandemic has thrown up some pretty significant challenges for his company.

It was not long after passing my guide's course in late 2000 that I found myself walking into Adventure Consultants' office. I was extremely nervous because I was about to ask if I could work for them. They had such a powerful reputation after their founders were killed on Mt Everest (Rob Hall) and Mt Dhaulagiri (Gary Ball). I was almost relieved that Guy was not there and I could only talk to his office manager Suze, the only person in the small office. She was friendly and we chatted before I left my resume in case they needed a guide. A few hours later I was stoked to get a call from Suze offering me a job on an expedition course with Dean, one of my assessors from the guide's course.

Treble Cone

After another winter in Utah we flew back to New Zealand and drove to Ohakune, packed our gear, rented out our home and drove down to Wanaka for the winter. I'd been offered the avalanche forecasting job on the ski patrol at Treble Cone Ski Area.

Taking on my new job was indeed a challenge. No one else had walked into that job without previously working at Treble Cone.

Some of the patrollers were really experienced, especially Gordie and Geoff, and they both helped me settle in. Gordie wanted me to reinstate the avalaunchers so I set about sighting them in.

One sunny afternoon Geoff and I were sighting-in an avalauncher after the ski area had closed, aiming the shot high up on what is called Towers Ridge. Unfortunately we had put a little too much gas in the chamber and the explosive had shot over the ridge into the valley behind. We heard the distant boom and looked at each other with concern. Our blood pressure ramped up a few more notches when a helicopter appeared behind the ridge and seemed to be flying around where our bomb had gone off, as though they were looking for someone. We packed up in a hurry and reluctantly headed home, dreading a phone call about missing skiers – thankfully it never came. It turned out the group of heli-skiers were looking to see if the bomb had caused an avalanche.

Sometimes explosives shot from the avalauncher don't detonate. A rod has to slide forward and hit a striking pin, but in soft snow the explosive can land quite softly and not go off. When this happened I had to ski over to where the bomb had disappeared into the snow, leaving a fist-sized hole, and carefully dig down until I could see the tail of the explosive. Then I'd place a hand charge next to it, light it and ski away, thus blowing up the dud round and making it safe to open the ski area. I loved it.

The snow safety job at Treble Cone lived up to its reputation. It challenged me and I enjoyed my first days of heli-skiing on my days off. My first ski guide's exam was later that winter and since by then I would be armed with the required skills, I considered applying to work in Antarctica. The jobs I was looking at involved working for the New Zealand Government at Scott Base. They all involved going away for several months, so I decided to keep my ambitions on hold a bit longer and see if I could get there as a guide instead. It would be more enjoyable and involve shorter trips.

After winter we drove to Ohakune to put our house on the market, rented a truck, loaded our gear and hit the road back to Wanaka. We would miss our friends in the Central North Island, but not the weather!

I spent the 2001-02 summer guiding for Adventure Consultants in their local operations. It was great working for such a prestigious company. They paid well and had a better food budget than the other companies (quite important for a climbing bum), plus there was the incentive for international expeditions.

We kept on rock climbing as much as possible and I really enjoyed putting up new routes. Climbing a new route in Wanaka required a lot of dirty, hard work, which I loved. You had to find the line, abseil down and crowbar off any big loose blocks, then climb up and down on your rope to madly scrub away the dust and loose rocks with a wire brush before you drilled the bolts for the protection and finally pulled the rope down and climbed it from the bottom without falling. Only then could you name it and receive credit in the guidebook. I completed around 15 new routes in Wanaka's excellent schist rock walls.

Starting an Iconic Festival

Later that autumn we flew to Australia for a six-week climbing trip, living off pasta and rice, sleeping in our tents and climbing all day – almost every day. I ended up in the Blue Mountains at a film festival called Escalade, which gave me the idea to start something similar in Wanaka.

So I planned our first film festival and called it the Wanaka Mountain Slide Festival. It was held on a beautiful spring Labour Weekend (October), the first fine weather weekend of the summer. It was actually way too fine to be inside. Eight speakers put on slide shows, which were all well attended. Jo collected the entrance fee cash in an ice cream container, while I introduced the speakers, organised the lights and ran the rest of the show. Our cash takings provided future holiday funds.

When a speaker who was flying in from Wellington was delayed because of fog, I had to think of something to fill the space. Guy lent us a DVD of Glenn Singleman's 1993 base-jumping film *Baseclimb*. Much to the enjoyment of the visitors and to my surprise, the film looked great on the big screen. This gave me the idea to start a film competition and change the timing of the festival to autumn, when the days are shorter and there is less to do in Wanaka.

Twenty years later the festival is going strong and is a core event in the Wanaka event calendar. In 2012 Jo and I turned the festival to a non-profit charitable trust with an eight-person board of trustees. It's also a registered charity and attracts thousands of people to Wanaka and Queenstown. We raise money for three causes we believe in: training youth in outdoor-adventure skills; helping people with disabilities buy sporting equipment; and supporting environmental projects. Every dollar is now accounted for, and it's become a six-month job to organise each year.

Late in 2002 we bought a section in a subdivision in Lake Hawea and in January 2003 we started building a house. We moved in with a camp stove for cooking and used the kitchen door as a bench. Our carpets were second-hand, there were no curtains, only one finished bathroom, and we painted the concrete floor to keep down the dust. We had loved Hawea ever since moving there and living in the late Dave Hiddleston's house in 1998.

Later that summer I received an invitation to join Guy and two other friends on a climbing trip to the Balfour Face, one of the most challenging and remote ice climbs in the country. Soon Guy and I were standing among avalanche debris under New Zealand's ice-climbing trophy, the Balfour Face of Mt Tasman (3497m). This icy 600m south face is in the centre of the Southern Alps, a good three-days' walk from the nearest road.

I'd eyed an unclimbed route in a photo in the guidebook. It was usually severely threatened by unstable hanging ice-cliffs, but in the late summer conditions, with global warming in our favour, it looked relatively safe, if steep and exposed.

Thirty minutes later Guy won the 'paper, scissors, rock' for the first lead. He scrambled into an ice-filled gully, which quickly steepened into a vertical frozen sheet of water ice. He set up an anchor and belayed me to his position hanging from the ice screws. I climbed the pitch with numb hands and at the anchors I screamed out in pain as my hands warmed up. This sensation is known as the 'screaming barfies' for that very reason. Guy smiled knowingly. Slowly the feeling of wanting to vomit passed, and I led on to the steep second pitch.

We climbed pitch after pitch, for hour after hour, and arrived at where we thought the angle would ease. But alas, steep ice led to overhanging bulges and vertical walls. I arrived beside my tired-looking partner. The 50m-high overhanging ice-cliff above him couldn't be avoided because it ran across most of the face. I slumped down on the welcome flat ground while we ate and drank in the late afternoon sunshine and pondered the problem above.

We had no sleeping bags and limited food, so as the sun started sinking closer to the Tasman Sea, without words Guy set off up the overhanging wall of ice. I would have happily slept right there and climbed it the following day. The climbing was tricky and awkward. Guy half aided and half ice-climbed the steep ramp in a fantastic display of sheer determination and grit. After breaking off the chandeliers dangling from the lip, he disappeared over the top. I felt desperate as I followed. My arms were cramping, I could barely lift them above my head. The ice was brittle and insecure, and I had no way of communicating with Guy. As I poked my head over the lip, I saw his big smile. He was on flat ground.

'Don't fall off, this anchor is shit,' he warned me. The snow was too soft to build a solid anchor, so he had buried his pack, tied me in and sat on it.

We didn't rest at all and charged straight off for the summit, gazing over our shoulders at the spectacular bright-red sun sinking into the Tasman Sea. Sunset from the top of the country's second highest mountain was a special experience. We barely stopped on the summit, exchanging a quick handshake before descending the north shoulder in the dusk.

We didn't mention it, but I'm sure we were both thinking that this very shoulder on Mt Tasman had killed some good friends of ours a few years before in an avalanche, including Dave Hiddleston.

We called the route Surreal Insomnia – the steepest and most sustained route on the face. I've known Guy for almost two decades now and back at the hut after the climb is still the only time I've ever seen him turn down a beer. He opted instead for a lie down and a well-earned rest.

9

VENTURING OVERSEAS

In the winter of 2003 Gordie and I were skiing an avalanche control route at Treble Cone. It was a white-out and we were skiing down Boundary Ridge with packs full of bombs. After a couple of shots we decided we couldn't see enough to be sure of our results so we abandoned the route. Without thinking, Gordie skied off towards the east side of the mountain, instantly setting off a large avalanche. As the snow broke like glass into metre-deep blocks it carried Gordie into the white-out and he disappeared.

Ski patrollers spend hours and hours practising for such a scenario. It's something we think about and talk about often. Yet I never expected it to be so terrifying. I used the radio to call the other patrollers and told them where we were and to send backup. Then I turned off my radio because I knew there would be all sorts of chatter as they mobilised a rescue team. If you can dig out an avalanche victim within 15 minutes, they statistically have an 80% chance of survival. The clock was ticking.

I turned my avalanche transceiver to search and started to follow the avalanche down the slope in complete white-out conditions. I could hear the signal of Gordie's transceiver, and it seemed as though he was about 30m away. I moved as quickly as I could, focusing on Gordie's position, and I was 15m away when I saw his head sticking out of the snow debris.

When I skied up to him he asked me to call the other patrollers to say I'd found him. His radio was still on and they were obviously panicking and trying to mobilise people to the site as quickly as possible. I did that, then had an idea. I started tickling his nose! He wasn't hurt, but he couldn't move because his arms were pinned under the avalanche debris. We both cracked up. I got my shovel out and started digging him out. He said, 'Take a photo,' so I did.

He was actually still standing upright with his skis on, and after 20 minutes of digging he was free. We skied back to the patrol shack, much to the relief of the other patrollers, who had also been given quite a fright.

Later in 2003 I received my first invitation to join an overseas expedition. I was to be a guide on a trip to Aconcagua in Argentina. It was one of the Seven Summits. These are the highest mountains of each of the seven continents: Everest, Aconcagua, Denali, Kilimanjaro, Vinson, Elbrus and Carstensz Pyramid.

On this expedition I found my niche in expedition electronics and spent hours and hours learning and using them to send dispatches to the company website. This included text and images so that friends and family could follow the expedition. I'm sure this skill has got me invitations on many more expeditions, because guides hate that stuff. It never works very well with old technology, fragile wires, poor satellite connections and short-lasting batteries.

The next of the Seven Summits I guided was the highest mountain in Europe, Mt Elbrus, which is in Russia. This was the first mountaineering experience for many in the group, so over a few days we had taught them the basic skills necessary to climb it. But you can't prepare someone for the gob-smacking beauty of seeing the sun slowly rise at 5am, turning the sky from black to deep blue, to pink, red and back to light blue. By mid-morning we were at the saddle between the two peaks having just entered the area where the sun was shining. The temperature rose dramatically. We stopped for the first decent rest of the day and put on sunblock and sunglasses, took off layers and drank and ate.

The final few hours took us up steep snow-covered slopes onto the summit plateau and finally the summit. There were cheers and hoots as numerous summit photos were snapped and then it was down, down, down. All the way to a snow groomer for a knee-saving ride down to the huts.

I was a combination of amused and alarmed when the snow groomer turned up. Two bikini-clad girls accompanied the driver – and they were all drunk. They got out, took some photos, then the driver took some belly-button shots of vodka from the giggling girls' bodies, before he grunted at us to get in the back. We went down the hill fast – he was driving at show-off speed.

10

SKIING THE PEAKS

I'm a bit of a dreamer. I love studying maps and looking for places to go, peaks to ski, valleys to explore. I enjoy studying the landscape, especially around home. We had played a film at the film festival in which a skier was attempting to ski Colorado's 54 14,000ft (3048m) mountains in a year. It was an awesome adventure set near where he lived.

I had what I thought was a brilliant idea. I contacted the Queenstown Lakes District Council and asked if it was possible to get a high-quality topographical map of our region. I was referred to the survey company which the council dealt with, and without too much fuss they sent me a DVD of a large file.

After hours studying the map I worked out there were 18 mountains within our boundary that were over 2500m high. I was stoked. Here was an adventure close to home. I believed that no one had ever discovered this before and I was positive no one had climbed them all – definitely not skied them, anyway. Even more exciting was that most of the mountains looked reasonably skiable.

So I tried to climb and ski them over the next few years. However, that didn't start out very successfully. Two years later

I'd attempted only three peaks and succeeded only on one. I was starting to understand the scale of the undertaking, yet I hadn't told anyone what I'd discovered. I wanted to have a crack at it before someone else did. But it could take 20 years at the rate I was going.

Then I spotted a competition. In 2010 The North Face company were offering an adventure grant – send in your idea for an expedition and you could win $10,000. This was the amount I needed to hire helicopters to access the snow line. I entered and I won! On my entry form I stated that I'd do it in a year, which I knew would be almost impossible. Regardless, I was up for giving it a try. I made a list of friends whom I could call at short notice and who could look after themselves in the mountains, scheduled very little work and waited for the winter.

I had already climbed and skied Mt Brewster, which was one of the peaks, with a good mate called Steve Moffat. Steve is one of the most genuine guys I've been lucky enough to become close friends with. His good nature, fun sense of humour, excellent climbing ability and easy-going attitude make him a fantastic adventure buddy. If I came up with an idea, which many friends would just laugh at, he'd be the one who would straightaway say he was keen to give it a crack.

We were climbing the difficult 500m steep ice-covered south face of Mt Douglas during our training for guides' qualifications. When you start guiding it's a bit like an apprenticeship; after you have completed the initial courses, you then work under the supervision of fully qualified guides, while you also do some of your own hard climbing preparing for your final exams. It took me seven years to complete the training.

We were halfway up the steep ice climb and I was climbing first, leading and placing ice screws in the hard blue ice. I was hanging off my arms, which were growing weaker and weaker as we climbed. Our ice axes were dug 4-5mm into the ice with cracks running out from the picks like shattered glass in a car window. It was scary stuff.

I was at what you call the crux of the climb – the most technically difficult part. When you are a couple of metres above your last ice screw you really have to control your imagination and keep calm. If you are relaxed and breathing, you can climb much more efficiently than if you are tense and gasping for breath. There I was, hanging from my ice axes, breathing deeply, but over-gripping, halfway through the difficulties. I knew my buddy Steve would be watching me carefully as he held onto the rope running through his belay device. That meant that if I fell, he'd hold me on the rope. From 20m above him I was digging up the courage and the energy to climb the next few metres past the crux and onto easier ground.

I looked over my shoulder and down at Steve to say, 'Watch me.' But my glance down didn't do anything to encourage me. To my horror, Steve had tied off the rope (so I was safe) and had his pants down around his ankles (no easy feat while he was hanging from the anchor) and was taking his morning dump. I closed my eyes, breathed deeply, cursed him and climbed on.

During the descent we had to go over another mountain called Glacier Dome. Near the bottom our route was cut off by an ice-cliff. We had to leave something behind to abseil off so that we could get down and back to the hut. I had half a foam pad in my pack, in case we got stuck outside for the night – we could sit on it and not freeze our backsides. So we compacted some snow into a sausage shape and rolled the foam pad around it, then we dug a slot in the soft snow and buried the burrito.

I clipped onto my rope and as I leant back on the anchor I said to Steve, 'What could possibly go wrong?' We lowered ourselves 10m to the snow below, then we jogged back to the hut happy with our climb.

Back to Mt Brewster. It took us three hours to carry skis, boots, climbing gear, sleeping gear, food and fuel from the road below to the hut. Tied to the top of my pack was my paraglider. It was a huge load. We stayed in the hut and then got up early to begin the climb. It was drizzling lightly when dawn broke and I asked Steve if he wanted to go back.

'Na, let's carry on for a bit,' he replied in his usual optimistic tone. Reluctantly I kept going. The weather never got any worse; it actually stopped raining and we climbed the steep snow ramp to the summit. After handshakes and man hugs we descended, strapped into our skis and blasted off down the glacier, all the way to the hut.

Back at the hut, I rigged up my paraglider, tied my skis across my back and loaded my heavy gear. But the wind was coming the wrong way, so I couldn't launch. I was about to give up when the wind changed direction briefly.

After one final check I sprinted towards the edge. My wing came over my head and I took off into the valley, soaring over the beech forest. It was something I'd dreamed about doing for years. I felt like James Bond or Inspector Gadget putting all my skills together to do it safely.

Steve cheered briefly, then realised he would have to walk down alone . . .

It had started out as fun, even though the weight in my pack was pulling me backwards. But then I noticed the wind in the trees – they were swaying wildly. I turned a full circle above the river to check the wind and realised it was strong. A paraglider flies at about 35km/hr. If the winds are stronger than that then you are flying backwards.

I lined up my landing in the riverbed, as close as I could to the trees for shelter. To my horror, I was coming down and moving backwards. Not a good situation. The fast-flowing river was just behind me. As I reached the shelter of the trees, my backward momentum slowed and I landed softly in the riverbed. I was stoked beyond belief as I rolled up my wing and walked a few hundred metres down the road to the car. We'd stashed a few beers in the river, and I was only starting my second one when Steve turned up, having run down the mountain as fast as he could. He was worried I was going to drink all the beer.

The adventure to climb and ski the other peaks wasn't easy, and completing them was often in doubt. I had the funds and a list of friends keen to participate in the adventures. My cameras were sorted out so I could film and photograph the trips. All I needed were the weather windows. This can be a rare thing in New Zealand with our often-unsettled weather.

By late September 2012 I'd still ticked off only three of the peaks because of the unseasonably bad weather. But now we were heading into the remote Snowdrift Range, where five of the peaks lay at the head of the Dart Glacier.

There we were – Lionel, Adrian and me – bivvying at the Whitbourn Saddle. It had been a few massive days getting there, having made a first ski descent of Mt Maoriri (2595m), and our food was almost out. We watched cloud roll over from the west. We needed perfect visibility to navigate down the route back to the Dart Glacier, or it would be a long, hungry, three-day hike.

The next day wasn't fine. The tops of the peaks were shrouded in cloud and there were strong winds, but we headed off up Mt Edward (2620m) anyway. Once we reached the summit, we did get the occasional clearance, enough to look down the steep east face, past avalanche debris, ice-cliffs and crevasses. It didn't look very promising, but we had picked out a route on our way in a few days before and thought we'd get down or, more accurately, *hoped* we'd get down.

We skied the east face on soft snow, ever closer to the big, towering ice-cliffs we knew were below. I traversed way out left, to where we'd thought the route went, but it ended in a 20m ice-cliff.

I turned around and came back. Lionel found a route down a steep gully below an active ice-cliff, which we followed in quick succession. We were trying not to rush, but we were fully aware a big hunk of ice could shear off at any moment and crush us like a fly on a car window. I traversed out left again, over big piles of car-battery-sized ice blocks, trying to put the danger overhead out of my mind, pushing left, around a steep corner, past gaping crevasses, under rocks until I saw the route down. I traversed more left, away from the ice-cliffs and down onto the Dart Glacier.

Yeeha! I'm not sure if the sweat on my forehead and shaking

hands were from the heat and exercise or the adrenaline. But either way, we high fived on the glacier and slumped down for a well-deserved rest as we gazed in astonishment at what we had just skied.

Lionel yelled, 'That was the dumbest thing I've done in a long time!' Then a big crack rang out and we jumped. Fortunately, we were safe – no ice came down that time.

It was 2014 when I finally climbed and skied Mt Ian, the final and most remote peak in the district. I went to the summit with Elliot, Steve and Tomas, skied it and then spent two more days getting back to Wanaka. I was stoked, but also a little sad that the journey was over. I'd become the first person to climb all the peaks. It took six years, with nine first ski descents and many, many great times, laughs and adventures with seriously good people.

11

SKIING IN A WAR ZONE

I started ski touring in Kashmir in northern India in 2012, and absolutely loved it from day one. This was not your usual ski resort. You had to look where you were skiing as there were occasional unused concrete mixers or even steel rebar used on construction sites sticking out of the snow. When I paid for my lift ticket by handing over Indian rupees the ticket seller looked at my money as if he'd never seen that currency before. Then he said, 'No change,' and wrote me an IOU so I could collect my change on the next run.

Afzal Guru was a Kashmiri terrorist sentenced to death over a 2001 plot to attack India's parliament. He was hung in February after his final clemency plea was rejected. Afzal had always denied plotting the attack, which left 14 dead. From then on India stepped up security and announced a day-and-night, shoot-on-sight curfew in Kashmir, where news of the execution was expected to spark unrest. It all sounded terrifying when we heard about it, but in Kashmir I was treated like a welcome guest. The locals looked out for us, as would the heavily armed Indian army soldiers.

Kashmir is in the far north of India. The border between India and Pakistan splits Kashmir in half, and saying they also don't like each other is an understatement. The Kashmiris, who are of Muslim descent, wanted independence, although they had learnt to tolerate the heavy Indian army presence. But they loved and welcomed tourists. It was difficult to walk anywhere in town without a group of Kashmiri men approaching and asking me if I was having a great time, where I was from, and who was my favourite New Zealand cricket player.

But it's not a place to injure yourself or get sick. I was there one year with a good friend called Dave and when he started eating the curry on the breakfast buffet I warned him. 'It'll only end one way,' I said, and it did. I suggested keeping his toilet paper outside the window, to keep it cool. After several days of dysentery, he also caught a chest infection and was seriously ill.

Reluctantly he headed for the Gulmarg Medical Clinic, with stomach cramping, severe dysentery, a tight chest and shortness of breath. The dimly lit clinic looked like a scene from a 1970s horror movie with wet floors, dim flickering light bulbs hanging from naked wires, dirty walls, a receptionist with a limp, a hunchback and a half-closed eye. Dave could hear water dripping and smell mould, but he was desperate for medical advice. He and the doctor sat at a school-like table, on school-style steel chairs while he asked Dave questions. Eventually he said he'd give him an injection, so Dave started rolling up his sleeve.

'No, no, my dear, the buttocks please,' said the doctor.

Dave swallowed hard, closed his eyes for a second, he couldn't believe it was happening . . .

At the top of the gondola at almost 4000m the air felt thin and you had to walk more slowly. Looking to the west you could see army bases scattered around the mountains and the faint outline of the Line of Control, a buffer zone with Pakistan and India on either side.

We stepped into our skis, ducked under the boundary fence and skied down the wind-swept ridge, past a miserable looking tented army camp with barking dogs. Two soldiers with AK47s ran over to stop us. They didn't speak much English, but it seemed they were worried about us setting off an avalanche. I said we were fine, but they insisted we go back to the gondola. I said no firmly and slid past them, on down the ridge. I told my reluctant friends to follow and they did as the soldiers screamed and waved their guns at us. I was fairly sure they wouldn't shoot, because that would have been very bad for the ski business, but I kept my head down and skied down the ridge.

From the top of the Drang Valley I could just make out Drang Village 1800m below. We chose a beautiful open bowl of untracked powder to drop into. The bowl slowly turned to tall, thin pine and paper trees and the skiing was magnificent in deep, light powder. Eventually, the valley narrowed and we joined other tracks, past a hydroelectric power plant and then up a rising traverse out of the river. The trail went over fences and through the roadless village of Drang.

Women were washing laundry, men were stocking firewood boxes and the kids were playing. They smiled and waved as we skied past, with the kids running up to ask for chocolate and money, but we only had smiles and laughter to give. Sadly some European tourists had started handing out chocolates, which in turn had encouraged begging.

'Who is your favourite cricket player?' many asked. We carried on with kids running behind us through the peaceful town with solar panels and satellite dishes scattered on rooftops. At the end of the trail, we crossed a long bridge and hiked the steps into Tangmarg, the town at the end of the Gulmarg road. After a tasty curry for lunch, it was a 30-minute taxi ride up to the Gulmarg hotel.

I find the Muslim culture relaxing and peaceful, although it can accelerate into a noisy riot quickly. They are genuinely friendly people and although they can look a bit rough to our Western eyes, a smile is always met with a smile and their sense of humour is not far away from ours. Part of the allure of Kashmir was that every day was an adventure, no ski tour was a given and it still draws me back year after year.

12

COMPLETING THE SEVEN SUMMITS

As I approached my late 40s, I took on less and less work for Adventure Consultants. It wasn't intentional, I just needed less work and wanted to concentrate more on ski guiding. Or, more importantly, I wanted to work less. Jo and I had paid off our mortgage and she worked hard as a real-estate agent. If we were both working long hours, we'd never see each other.

It saddens me when I see people my age, such as old friends, working long, long hours, spending huge amounts of money on living, expensive toys, expensive holidays, expensive habits, which cause them to have to work longer hours. Their health worsens, they put on weight and they eventually have nothing to do when they aren't working. Some of my wealthiest friends, in my eyes, are the ones who work less, have less money, but are doing the things they want to do. Not thinking they need more, but content with what they have. I've tried to emulate this.

It wasn't until 2019 that I finally got a chance to complete the Seven Summits. I found out you could paraglide off Mt Kilimanjaro, so for my 50th birthday I set about organising a trip to try just that with four paragliding friends.

Ever since I was a kid I'd dreamt of flying. When I was on a mountain top I'd wish for a way to safely fly down to the bottom the way a cartoon character in a kids' film might. Paragliding gives you that ability, and hiking up to fly down also provided excellent fitness as I got older, saving the knees from long painful steep descents.

Nothing quite compares with a cool autumn day's hike up a mountain that I can see from home. Climbing high above the lake, sweating profusely from the weight of the glider on my back, lungs heaving, legs burning. Getting to the top then taking a minute to enjoy the views, eventually unrolling the wing and taking off into the smooth air. Floating downwards, slowly turning big circles, feeling that weightlessness associated with skiing and kitesurfing, that feeling of floating on air, the feeling of effortless movement, the euphoria.

Our paragliding group went to Tanzania a week early to fly and explore the lesser-travelled national parks. We found a village on top of a 1000m-high plateau and took off over the African plains. I flew for almost 50km that day. When the winds became a little too strong, I selected a village to land near, hoping there'd be somewhere to have a cold drink once I landed (our jeep had to drive three to four hours down from the mountain to collect us).

I lined up my landing in a field near a village with several people working in the afternoon heat. Just as I was about to land, a dust devil popped up and caused me to accelerate. When my feet touched the ground, I ran as fast as I could, but I couldn't keep up. I landed on my face in an explosion of dust. My paraglider carried on and crashed in front of me. I was so excited about my flight that I rapidly stood up. Covered in dust and smiling widely, I gave the thumbs up to the shocked family standing just a few metres away.

They must have wondered what had happened. A crazy white man had fallen from the sky. They'd never seen paragliders in that part of Tanzania. I was an instant celebrity. Around 250 villagers, mostly kids, came running to see me, standing millimetres from my paraglider, shoulder to shoulder, smiling and laughing. The kids were less shy and would yell basic English phrases such as 'What is your name?' I loved that experience, rolling up my paraglider while they watched on in bewilderment.

Just then Chris, one of the other pilots, landed. For a few minutes the crowd forgot about me and ran screaming towards Chris. We were both laughing and taking photos, lapping up the experience. A few locals latched on to me and protected me from the others. Everyone was trying to get closer to get a good look at us. I asked a young woman if there was somewhere we could get a cold drink, and she said yes.

We walked as if we were movie stars, with half the crowd walking in front and the other half behind. There was singing and laughing. Everyone seemed to be proud to be walking with us. I couldn't believe how cool it was. The Tanzanians are good-looking people too. The young lady escorting me gave me a shy smile and suggested quietly she could be my wife.

We found the town's shop and gently pushed through the crowd to the cool, shady interior, which was like a small living room with a table and two chairs. One older boy stood at the door with a big stick and was ordered by the shop keeper to threaten any kids who tried to come inside. They sat just out of reach and stared at us, smiling when we caught their eye. The store keeper had cold beers and a fan. It was a welcome relief from the scorching African heat. We rested for a bit, sent a message to our friends and relaxed for a couple of hours while our driver found his way to us.

The other guys had landed in less populated areas but had similar fun experiences. We were the only ones who had landed near cold beer, and we took the prize for the best flight.

A few days later we met up with Jo and eight others to climb Mt Kilimanjaro. It's a fun hike, and I enjoyed the climb. It was a mostly stress-free trek without the need for ice axe and crampons. As always with these trips, the main highlight was the interaction with the local Tanzanian staff. They were really amazing people, happy and easy going, and would break into song with any excuse.

We summited around 7am and local porters carried up our paragliders. It would have been the most spectacular flight if we'd had the right conditions, a 5000m descent landing right in

Moshi just a few hundred metres from the hotel bar. But the wind was blowing from the wrong direction, so it was an easy but sad decision to walk down. We ended up running down the 3000m to the road end in one long day so that we could spend the following day paragliding nearby.

It was really cool to complete the Seven Summits. Records haven't been well kept, but I believe I am about the eighth or ninth New Zealander to do so.

Skiing the Seven Continents

Skiing the Seven Continents is a relatively new adventure for skiers and boarders. It's a great way to meet the local people, experience the food and learn about the culture of each continent. There's nothing too serious about exploring the globe and exploring different regions while enjoying good turns. The seven continents are: Australasia, South America, North America, Asia, Europe, Africa and Antarctica. Each of the continents in the world is unique with its own culture, languages, climate, geographic features and identity.

On 21 February 2020 I skied the African continent, 364 days after skiing in Gulmarg on the Asian continent. Between those two dates I skied in Antarctica, North and South America, New Zealand and Europe. So I completed skiing on the Seven Continents in just under a year. I suspect Jo and I were New Zealand's first woman and man to ski and snowboard on the Seven Continents, although I can't see any knighthoods or damehoods in our futures.

One day in Morocco we were walking past a resting camel covered in desert dust with its wet disgusting foot-long tongue hanging out the side of its mouth when it let go a huge fart. My friend Shane burst out laughing.

'They look so funny,' he said.

'They look like camels,' I replied with a wink.

The snow line in Morocco was 300m above the road, so our local guide loaded all the skis, boards and boots onto a mule, while we easily hiked the track, obsessing about the high peaks above. We were looking for solid faces, or even patches of snow. There wasn't much.

But we made it to the snow line, exchanged runners for ski boots, mule for skins and made our way up the mountain. There was no snow on the sunny aspects but 5-10cm of fresh winter snow on the shady slopes. As soon as we reached a high point, we ripped off our skins, locked down the heels and took off, ripping up turn after turn down a tongue of snow back to our waiting mule.

Part Two

Escaping Catastrophe

13

AN AVALANCHE THAT SHOULD HAVE ENDED IT ALL

I was tightly packed in a tomb of snow. My mouth was stretched wide open and packed full of snow. My eyes were also wide open but seeing only cold blackness. Every muscle in my body was trying to move, but I was gripped by the concrete-like snow packed around my body. I could sense that I was completely upside down, as if I was doing a headstand. I hate headstands!

I couldn't even take a breath. I wasn't afraid, but I was briefly angry. How could I be so stupid? Then I thought of my family. I felt sad. I started saying goodbyes. I knew I'd been swept into a large crevasse by an avalanche and that my friend would not be able to find me in time.

I was resigned to the fact that I was going to die here, cold and lonely . . .

Although I didn't realise it at the time, my fascination with avalanches had started four years earlier in Canada in 1991 when I was 21.

We were skiing at Mt Norquay in Banff National Park in a snowstorm when we came upon a beautiful steep slope with fresh snow. It was fenced off. We were undeterred and three of us, me, Ollie and Phil, climbed over the barrier and started hiking up the slope, oblivious that it was a dangerous avalanche path. We hadn't gone far when we heard shouting from the ski patrol below. Four or five guys were waving frantically at us. I assumed we were in trouble, so we put on our skis and skied down slowly.

Just before we reached them, we straight-lined it and raced past them at full speed, confident that we could make a high-speed escape. We flew down the ski trail, ducking past skiers, flying off the rollovers at Olympic downhill-like speeds (in our minds). Phil ducked into the trees just after a corner and got away, while Ollie and I arrived at the bottom of the run. But we had forgotten that we'd have to ride the chairlift to get back to our car and escape. The ski patrol had kept up with us easily and had radioed ahead to tell the lift attendant to stop the lift. We stood there as if we were dummies, embarrassed to have been caught.

I had no idea about avalanches or the ski patrol. It was a quick introduction, followed by us being arrested by an unimpressed sheriff and then a court appearance. I was intrigued by these mountain workers who studied and blew up avalanches with explosives, rescued injured people and chased skiers who broke the law. Little did I know this would lead me into a lifetime career of ski patrolling, avalanche instruction and mountain guiding.

I turned up in court on the assigned date, while my friend Ollie scarpered and left the country. The judge thanked me for turning up and fined me $200. I didn't have enough money to pay the fine, so I drove to the airport, left our old Oldsmobile car idling outside, walked inside, checked in, then flew to England.

The next time I came across avalanches was the following winter in Austria, where I'd got a job washing dishes. We'd mostly ski off-piste, and in Austria that meant out of bounds, but not closed out of bounds as in Canada, so there was no risk of arrest. It was

'Use at your own risk' out of bounds, or backcountry. As we skied massive bowls and mountain faces, I still had absolutely no idea what avalanches were.

There were large 5m-high steel-frame avalanche barriers built on the more dangerous slopes, and the snow built up behind them, forming 'ski jumps'. I'd ski the steepest slopes, in the biggest storms, jumping over the avalanche barriers with my friends, who also had no idea how dangerous that was. We had no avalanche rescue gear and we were good enough skiers to expose ourselves to real danger.

On one occasion, I jumped over a barrier, landed with a crash on my hip and came to a sudden halt. The snow below my feet cracked and slid away down the mountain. It built up speed and momentum and when it hit the old established trees below, their trunks snapped. I shrugged my shoulders and carried on, a bit gutted that all the soft powder snow had gone and that the snow left behind was hard. I had absolutely no idea I'd almost killed either myself or, even worse, someone below.

This did spark an interest in learning, though, and back in New Zealand I signed up for a seven-day professional avalanche management course which was also one of the prerequisites for getting a job ski patrolling. The avalanche course was at Temple Basin Ski Area in the South Island. It was to be a great week of ski touring, something I'd never tried. Ski touring is when you have a binding with a releasable heel, and you attach sticky skins to the base of your skis. The skin allows the ski to slide forward, not backward, enabling you to walk uphill almost effortlessly. Then once you are at the top of a run, you take off the skins, lock your heels back down, and ski the run in normal ski mode.

My brain was like a sponge and I became transfixed by the snow science, safe travel and rescue techniques which we learnt that week. I found it fascinating that you could study the snow layers, crystal shape and size, temperatures and density, then figure out if an avalanche was likely.

Later that winter of 1994, armed with my new avalanche qualification and pre-hospital emergency care course, I started ski patrolling.

At the end of the winter I booked a flight to America, to a little-known ski area called Snowbasin in Utah. I was hoping for a job on the ski patrol, but in those days Kiwis weren't eligible for work visas. I rented a room in a house with two other Kiwi ski bums, John and Jamie, and two American ski patrollers, Frank and Brandon. I'd met Brandon in Ohakune the winter before.

We bought season passes and skied every day, rehydrating with the famous Utah beer, which had a distressingly low alcohol content. I hung out with the ski patrol and befriended Tim, the manager. I volunteered for the ski patrol, and although it wasn't technically legal, Tim was okay with it. Their ski patrol members were relatively young and inexperienced and my avalanche skills and enthusiasm for digging snow profiles were useful. I gave lectures to the other team members on snow science and avalanche forecasting.

I'd been there for a few weeks when I came up with a scheme in which I would work for patrollers on their days off. They would state on their pay sheets that they had worked, and when they'd been paid they'd give me the cash, minus their tax. Again, Tim turned a blind eye to this despite it being highly illegal. In the meantime, we were trying to figure out a way to get me a work permit.

Not long after, the American National Ski Patrol Association struck up a deal with immigration for a ski patrol exchange programme. If a resort in New Zealand employed an American patroller, the American's place of employment could obtain a work visa for a New Zealander. In 1995 I successfully established the Turoa Ski Resort and Snowbasin Ski Resort exchange programme, which remains in place today after more than 25 years. A vast number of ski patrollers from each country have benefitted from working abroad and learning and sharing skills.

I loved working at Snowbasin because there was a lot of avalanche study to undertake. I dug snow profiles, checking the snow crystals, temperatures and their stability. It's the type of experience you can't get working in New Zealand.

Being a mischievous Kiwi, I also played a few pranks.

Ski patrollers spend many hours practising the important skill of avalanche rescue. We'd bury an avalanche transceiver. Then we'd record the time it took for each of us to find it. An avalanche transceiver is an electronic device worn on your body; if you get buried in an avalanche the people on the surface, with good training, can locate you very fast. Any more than three minutes and you'd be put on the beer-fine list.

I recall one occasion when I decided to play a trick. I climbed a tree in the large stand of pine trees near a burial site and hung the avalanche transceiver as far out on a branch as I could reach. Then I called in and said the site was set up, then I skied off.

I had forgotten about my trick, but then halfway through my lunch I remembered. The radio had been very quiet, and I became suspicious that something was up. I hastily put on my skis and headed down to check. When I got there, I felt sheepish. Three patrollers had dug a hole about 5m wide and 2m deep. They were all stripped down to their thermal tops and sweating madly from the effort of digging. From my position about 30m away I could see the transceiver they were looking for, hanging from the tree above their heads.

The signal from a transceiver doesn't tell you if it is up or down, but you usually assume it is down. Then one of the patrollers sat down in a huff and I saw him glance up into the tree. I knew he'd spotted the transceiver when he let out a yell. I turned quickly and skied down the mountain and never looked back.

After winter had finished, five patroller friends and I rented a space-wagon van and drove 12 hours north to Sunshine Village Ski Area in Canada. The resort I worked at in New Zealand also had an exchange with Sunshine Village and we'd been invited to their end of season party. We turned up in Banff and enjoyed the skiing and the subsequent party.

A few days later we headed back to Utah through the US border. I was conscious of my New Zealand passport, so I told the driver, Brendon, to say I'd only been skiing in Utah, not working. At the border the customs official asked where we were from.

'Utah,' replied Brendon. 'And one guy from New Zealand.'

'What was he doing in Utah?' asked the customs official.

'Working with us,' said Brendon.

My heart sank. I was hauled out of the van and taken to a holding cell with two chairs and a small table. Handcuffs sat on the table between me and the angry-looking customs official. I did not have a work visa and he asked me why I was working in Utah.

'I was only skiing,' I said as calmly as I could. 'My friend was just joking with you. He obviously didn't realise how serious his comment was.'

Without replying, the customs official left the room and went outside to the van. Everyone had given Brendon a hard time about his reply and when the official asked him again, he replied that he was just joking and didn't realise his joke wasn't funny.

Meanwhile I was waiting nervously. I'd set up the exchange for the following year and didn't want to get banned from America. Thankfully when the customs official came back, he said our stories matched and I was free to enter the country. We drove south away from the border with all of us laughing at what had happened.

With all my snow safety and avalanche training I felt in 1995 that I was ready for my final avalanche exam. This was a difficult pass-or-fail course in which you were tested on various skills. It was to take place in Queenstown in July, so Murray and I drove down. There were a lot of older, expert mountain guides on the course. They had recently joined the International Federation of Mountain Guides (IFMGA) and needed to do the course. I came second and was well pleased with my achievement. It was time to head back to Mt Ruapehu and the ski patrol.

Later that winter I was also offered a job teaching a seven-day avalanche course in the South Island at Broken River Ski Area. Nights were spent lecturing and days running ski tours and skills in the snow. After the job finished, I met my friend Kane for a mountaineering trip to Aoraki/Mount Cook National Park.

Flying into the head of the 25km-long Tasman Glacier in early August in an old ski plane was bloody exciting for a young ski bum. The mountains are absolutely huge, soaring 3000m above Aoraki/Mt Cook Village, and covered in many metres of winter snow.

We were wedged into the back of the three-seater plane full of food and climbing and ski gear. Faces were glued to the windows, our eyes wide open, wearing broad but nervous smiles. The pilot pumped a large lever that pulled up the wheels and the landing skis came down. He revved the plane's engine loudly then dived steeply down at the smooth-looking Tasman Glacier. The nose came up just in time and we bumped roughly onto the snow then bounced again before coming to an uneventful stop. The engine was shut off. Cool air and silence greeted us as we stepped from the plane.

From the drop-off we skinned high above the Kelman Hut and set about digging ourselves a snow cave in the deep, cold winter snow. A snow cave is when you dig into the snow surface and hollow out a dome-like structure. We carved out a bed on each side then a cooking table. We poked an avalanche probe out through the roof to create a vent and blocked the small door with our packs. It was cosy.

That was my first experience digging and living in the snow. It was great fun not just surviving winter nights in New Zealand's high mountains but being comfortable and adapting to the elements. I was amazed that we could build a shelter under the snow surface (even though I suffer mild claustrophobia) that could survive the nastiest storm Mother Nature could throw at it.

Kane had completed a 10-day mountaineering course, so he knew a lot more than me. He knew we should shape the ceiling round so water drops ran down the sides, and dig a vent for the carbon monoxide to escape. I helped to select a site out of the avalanche path. We had to melt snow for water, insulate ourselves from the snow 'beds' and dry our ski boot liners in our sleeping bags. Life became very simple and all our senses were alive. Food became key because if we were not skiing, we'd be eating.

The best thing about it was the freedom to explore the various ski runs and the lovely winter snow. There were shallow bowls, steep faces and huge valleys to explore. It was like being a kid in a candy store!

It was freezing, though, and we were only really in the snow cave to avoid paying fees at the nearby Kelman Hut. We skied to the hut in the evening and listened to the weather forecast, then skinned back up to camp for the night. That only lasted a few nights because the hut then became empty. We moved in and never answered the radio, thus avoiding paying the fees. I never felt guilty about not paying. I really had no money, and I still think young Kiwis should get free access to the mountain huts to encourage them into the mountains. It being mid-winter, the national park was completely empty. There wasn't another soul to be seen. The huts without heating, the short days and the high avalanche danger were probably the reason.

I was like a sponge, learning as much as I could from Kane, even though he didn't know very much either because much of his mountaineering course had been done in bad weather. But I knew about the snowpack, so we thought we'd be right. I believed I knew what I was doing, but I was about to learn a tough lesson.

It was mid-winter; we had been living in the snow for six days and there was still fresh powder snow everywhere. It was our last day on the glacier and we wanted to ski the formidable-looking steep south-east face of Mt Green (2847m). The weather was deteriorating. The wind had increased and was blowing a lot of snow around.

After a couple of hours climbing, I began worrying about the steep slope above us. I said to Kane, 'It looks like that ridge we want to climb is too dangerous.'

Too much snow was being deposited on it and it presented a very real avalanche danger. It was a steep snow arête leading up to a plateau below the face that we wanted to ski, and there was no avoiding the bulging snow ridge. To a skier it looked so pristine and inviting, but I suspected an avalanche lurked there.

We decided to turn back and ski the fantastic-looking slope

below us. Kane normally skied first, since I was more experienced with avalanche rescue. So off he went, skiing carefully. The snow looked good until near the bottom where he set off a small avalanche, 15m across by 10cm deep. It wasn't a big slide, and he was able to ski off to the side where he waited under the safety of an ice cliff to watch me come down.

Avalanche activity is a sure sign of avalanche danger, and I should have turned back and gone another way. But it was only a small slide and it stopped well before the small crevasse near the foot of the slope. (Second warning: a crevasse is what's called a terrain trap as an avalanche will bury you deeply in it.) I started the descent and found the skiing very enjoyable.

About halfway down I jumped over a small bergschrund, the crevasse which forms at the edge of glaciers, where I noticed the snow was a little stiffer.

At that moment the ground started moving under me. Avalanche! I looked behind me and saw the top of a metre-deep avalanche uphill from me. I had no chance of jumping off the back of the avalanche (something I'd done before). When I looked right then left, my heart sank. I was in serious trouble. The slab was 60 to 80m across, and I was in the middle.

'Watch out!' shouted Kane, fruitlessly. I started accelerating quickly.

Let me explain my situation another way. Imagine you are standing in the middle of a tennis court that for some reason is on a 40-degree angle. Then, without warning, it starts falling down the hill fast. Put some skis and boots on your feet and a heavy pack on and then try to get off the court. You'd have about two or three seconds. If that doesn't sound hard enough, just when you think you're making progress the one-metre-thick tennis court starts breaking into pieces the size of a dinner table and the gaps between these pieces suck you down into the snow.

There was no time to panic. I knew from my training that I had to fight for my life. There was no time to yell, I was concentrating. It was as if I was treading water. As I tried to stay on top of the snow and inch my way to the side, the earth collapsed under me.

It went dark as I felt myself falling. I hit something hard which winded me, but it collapsed and I kept falling. I hit something else and at the same instant the snow pounded down on top of me. Imagine lying in a 2m-deep grave and have a dump truck tip a few cubic metres of heavy dirt over you.

My training instantly kicked in and I started thrashing my head back and forth to make an air pocket. But I could only move it about 2cm. I was choking on the snow jammed in my mouth. I tried to chew it and spit some out. My left arm was stuck straight out, but my right hand was next to my chin, so I was able to scoop the snow from my mouth with a finger. I was about to pass out when I cleared my mouth of snow with the only part of me that could move – my finger. At last I was able to take a breath. Whew!

However, I was in a grave predicament. It was dark and I couldn't move. I yelled to Kane. There was no reply. It was like yelling into a pillow that was being held over my face. I knew it wouldn't be long before I passed out due to the lack of air. The heat and moisture from your exhaled breath form an ice cone around your head and block the air from penetrating. It is like drowning. Drifting into a deep sleep, never to regain consciousness. I said to myself goodbye and sorry to Mum, Dad and Jon, hoping somehow that they'd hear me. I thought about my girlfriend Jo.

Normally Kane would have been able to find me in two or three minutes by using our avalanche transceivers. But I had been swept into a deep crevasse, maybe 10 to 20m under the surface.

My mind was racing. I was angry with myself for getting into such a situation. I should have known better. I tried to move my legs and a surge of hope hit me – I could move my right foot. I wriggled my torso and saw light creep along my body. My other arm was alongside my body and my hand was near my knee, so I frantically dug away the snow towards my foot. I was almost there, but I was digging upwards and the snow collapsed back in on me, once again filling my mouth. Again, I had to chew and spit out snow.

I must get out, I thought, as once more I started digging. Ever so slowly I was able to dig a hole big enough to enable me to undo the shoulder straps on my pack then wriggle my body up and out of my coffin of snow and ice.

I was out! I couldn't believe it. I knew that 99% of the time you could not dig yourself out of such a burial. I was relieved but also exhausted, and now the fear started to take hold. I wasn't completely free yet though, I had to keep concentrating.

I was in a cave of ice with an opening at one end. I leaned forward. That's when I heard Kane. He was abseiling down the vertical walls of the crevasse, with the avalanche transceiver bleeping loudly and a shovel in his hand. Our eyes met and at once the stress fell away as we both knew I'd survive.

He smiled broadly and said, 'How are your undies?' in typical fashion. I couldn't muster up any reply and just dropped my forehead to the snow. I took a couple of deep breaths.

Somehow I had broken through the side wall of the crevasse and landed on a small snow bridge 10m down. The hole which I had been tossed through was barely half the size of a doorway; I hit it at about a 60-degree angle. The main crevasse was 20 to 30m deep and filled with debris up to 10m from the surface. If I had been 50cm to the left or right I would have bounced off the icy crevasse wall and ended up at the bottom buried under all that snow. It would have taken Kane hours to dig me out — if it was at all possible.

I climbed up the rope that he had secured while he looked for my gear. Once I was on the surface I collapsed on the ground. Overwhelmed by emotion, I cried my heart out. Then the physical pain set in. My leg and back ached so much I thought I might vomit. Kane found my skis and poles, but I'd lost my hat, gloves, sunglasses and goggles. They'd been ripped off me during the avalanche.

We didn't talk much. I was shivering and Kane was busy loading his pack up with as much of our gear as he could, leaving my pack lighter.

Luckily I could ski, but we were a long way from any help. But we never even considered calling in a rescue. It just didn't enter our minds. I didn't think I was hurt that badly and in those days self-reliance was much more of an ethic. We were alone and we had to look after each other. Kane even stamped 'OK' out in the snow in case someone saw the avalanche from the air and sent in a rescue team. I was hot, but also shaking uncontrollably. We needed to make it to De La Beche Hut before dark – it was about 7km away down the Tasman Glacier.

Our next mistake was trying to traverse directly to the hut. We ended up on steep, dangerous and slippery rock slabs covered in shallow snow. Loose rocks and scree made it almost impossible as we scratched and scraped our way to the hut. Four hours later, just on dark, it started to rain as we stumbled into the hut.

We rested the following day because I was stiff and sore and could hardly move. Lucky for me the two friendly Aussies staying in the hut shared their painkillers – we didn't have a first aid kit. After hearing our story one of them reached out with a handful of Panadol, saying, 'Take them all, mate, you are one lucky bastard.'

The next day it was time to leave. A storm was coming, and we weren't sure how long it would last. The Aussies were keen on sharing a taxi to come up the snow-covered Tasman Valley Road as far as it could, reducing the distance to travel from 27km to about 20km. I agreed gladly. Regardless, it was still a long day. My back ached, and I wasn't able to pick up my pack by myself. Kane had to lift it onto my back for me. I ran out of painkillers around midday and my leg was sending up sharp stabs of pain with every step. I wanted to lie down and give up. But I made myself think of other places, and other things, such as chocolate or a hot shower, to keep myself going. I mentally removed myself from the situation and relied on instinct.

For 10 hours Kane broke the trail and kicked steps in the deep snow for me. There was still a metre of snow in Aoraki/Mt Cook Village, but we finally made the waiting taxi just after dark. There was a day shelter in the Village that we slept in, but the water was frozen so we went thirsty, sleeping on the picnic tables to get away from the damp, frozen concrete floor.

The next day we drove to Christchurch Public Hospital, where I had my back and leg x-rayed. Thankfully my leg was just bruised, but my back was broken, a stable-hairline fracture of the T1 vertebrae. The doctor looked at me over the x-ray and said, 'You must have hit quite hard to fracture a vertebrae like that.' I don't think he had any idea of the power of the avalanche forces.

I asked him, 'What's the treatment for that sort of injury?'

He replied that there was no danger of nerve damage and that I should just keep moving as I usually would.

Kane and I decided we'd drive four hours north to Takaka and camp at Paynes Ford. It was a great place to go rock climbing and heal. Our discussions were pretty short, we were both quiet people. Something along the lines of:

'Should we go to Paynes?'

'Yea.'

'You wanna drive?'

'Sure.'

And we were off on our next adventure.

Hanging from rock faces actually stretched my back muscles and helped with my recovery. I never even thought about physio in those days. That would come the next time I broke my back – 25 years later.

14

A VOLCANO ERUPTS

I was staring wide eyed at the scene in front of me. It was so weird and unexpected that my brain was taking a moment to compute. The mountain was erupting? There was no sound, just a catastrophic explosion upwards. Raw power. Deep black rocks mixed with ash and pure white pluming clouds of steam and gas. I bent my neck backwards and my eyes focussed on large projectiles the size of cars and fridges hurtling upwards, thousands of metres above me.

Then in a microsecond it computed – the mountain WAS erupting, and those rocks were about to start coming down on us . . .

I'd been working on the Turoa Ski Area ski patrol for a couple of winters. Turoa, along with the Whakapapa Ski Area, sits on the sides of Mt Ruapehu, the biggest mountain in the North Island and an active volcano. I just never thought *that* active!

It had been a good winter with loads of snow and plenty of good weather. Rumours that Mt Ruapehu was becoming more active were circulating. The Department of Conservation had released a hazard warning that was so intriguing we went to have a look. It was an exciting prospect, looking into the bowl of a live volcano. The 'hazard warning' pretty much just said the risk was higher and people should keep their distance, I think it said 1km from the crater. For me it was like a flyer advertising a free live-volcano viewing.

Jo and I headed off from the top of the highest ski lift, the High Noon T-bar, for the 45-minute climb to the summit. Neither of us thought we were doing anything dangerous and we chatted casually. We'd only been dating a short while and everything was rosy.

'It looks like all the ice has fallen off the summit rocks,' I said to Jo. They were usually covered with 60-90cm of rime ice, which grew in the direction of the prevailing wind.

When we reached the summit, we could see that the ice hadn't fallen off – it was actually covered in black ash. We could hear the water running quietly behind the black covering. There must have been a small eruption during the last storm and snow hadn't covered the ash on the rocks.

We skied into the crater and decided not to go too close to the bubbling lake. It was a little spooky being inside the crater with the lake on one side and the high mountain face we'd just skied down on the other. We were trapped if anything happened. The lake appeared to be boiling, like the water in a frying pan that is ready for your poached eggs. There were bubbles coming from underneath and you could see currents as the water moved about. Occasionally there were small explosions of mud and water shooting up 20-50m into the air. It was like a magnified version of what I'd seen at Rotorua's hot mud pools.

We climbed west out of the crater then up a peak called Paratetaitonga and spent a few hours taking photos and enjoying the show. We felt relaxed here, being further away. But it was then that we became alarmed when we saw that a group of people had hiked from Whakapapa Ski Area and were standing very close, too close to the crater lake, looking into it from the top of the 20m ice cliffs on the water's edge. They were too far away to yell to and we could only look on in disbelief.

Jo said to me, 'I can't believe those guys are standing there. On that cliff edge.'

We didn't want to stay and watch so we headed off home in the opposite direction. On our way back to Turoa we enjoyed perfect turns down the Mangaturuturu Glacier on smooth untracked snow with views over native bush all the way to Mt Taranaki and the Tasman Sea.

The next day I was back at work on the mountain. It was 25 September 1995. I was on patrol and there was a solid line of people climbing to the summit to look at the bubbling lake. By 4pm the lifts had closed, and most people were coming down the mountain. But there were several still at the crater rim, visible from the ski resort below.

At the end of the day the patrol always does a 'sweep' of the mountain, checking for any injured or lost skiers or snowboarders.

I was on the far-west sweep at an area called the Eagle's Beak with another patroller, Gary. The sweeping patrollers work together across the entire width of the ski area, sweeping down to pre-determined spots and calling in via radio as they wait for the other patrollers to reach the same level.

I was looking at the people by the summit, about a kilometre away, when an almighty eruption occurred – with no sound. Rocks the size of fridges and cars, and ash were hurled several thousand metres into the air. It was such a surreal sight, especially because there was no sound. It took a split second for me to register that the mountain was erupting.

The people at the crater rim were ducking and running away – ants in comparison with the rocks that were spewing from the volcano. We couldn't see the 20m-high wall of water and ash, the lahar, which was now flowing down the mountain a kilometre to the west.

I was craning my neck looking at the rocks hurtling skywards, then slowly spinning and falling towards us. Then Gary and I looked at each other briefly, both with horrified looks on our faces.

He yelled, 'Go!' then we turned our skis to face down the slope and straight-lined it down the mountain as quickly as possible. We were expecting rocks to land around us – or even on us – at any second and we wanted to put some distance between us and the eruption.

We skied quickly through the Organ Pipes, where there were two patrollers starting to ski a toboggan with a patient on it out of the gully. It didn't look as if they'd seen the eruption and as we were expecting lava and lahar to start chasing us down the gullies, we yelled out to them. 'Hurry up, the mountain is erupting.' I was still feeling terrified and my heart was racing. They were uphill from our position and I felt helpless. I skied out of the gully so at least I'd be safe and could come back to help them if they got injured. When we talked later they did admit they thought we were having them on until they got out of the gully and looked back at the smouldering summit.

On the other side of the Organ Pipes I stopped to look back. I needed to see how close the rocks and the lahar were. It was then that I noticed rocks landing around the summit, close to the top. The wind was blowing from the south, away from Turoa. It was okay to breathe a sigh of relief.

The mountain was still erupting ash and steam several thousand metres into the sky, but we no longer felt threatened. The people around the summit all seemed to be skiing down, having escaped the eruption.

Further down, the carpark was full of cars and people, enjoying the show. After completing the sweep, we took off our ski boots, grabbed a beer and sat on the helipad to enjoy the surreal view of the continuing eruption. There were 10 patrollers and we laughed and joked with each other about how terrified we'd briefly been. How we thought the mountain might collapse into molten lava. We weren't scared any more, but we certainly had been for a few moments.

I guess it was a kind of post-eruption high. It was a sunny, warm afternoon, the whites of the snow gaining colour as the sun dipped into the Tasman Sea. White and grey steam and gas continued to bellow in a giant mushroom-shaped cloud rising thousands of metres above us like a giant nuclear explosion.

We found out later that the lahar had come down through the Whakapapa Ski Area's far-west T-bar lift, right where the queue, which had luckily closed 30 minutes before, would have been. The fast-flowing ash and water would have swept away the skiers standing in the lift line. Miraculously no one had been near the crater rim as they had been the day before and there were no injuries or fatalities, despite over 5000 people being on the mountain that day.

Both ski resorts were closed the next day so that the danger could be assessed. With nothing else to do we went for a drive around the mountain, taking photos and enjoying more views of the eruption. When we got back to Ohakune half of the locals had packed up and left; the other half had brought their couches and beach chairs into the streets where there was the best possible view.

Ash had blown over to the Whakapapa field and covered the snow in a black sand-like substance. Turoa was still clean, so the ski resort opened with the mountain still erupting above it. The Department of Conservation had made an exclusion zone around the top and many of our lifts were outside this. Management armed us with gas masks, then we opened the lifts to the few hardy skiers and boarders who had come to enjoy themselves. Many came just to get a close-up look at the eruption. We felt intimidated being up there having heard reports the gas would turn your lungs inside out, but we put on brave faces and did what we were told.

I'm pretty sure an employer would never send workers to such a workplace these days. One of the ski patrollers said to me, 'We shouldn't be here,' and quietly walked off the mountain, handing in his resignation.

When the wind eventually changed direction and poisonous gases (carbon monoxide and sulphur dioxide) drifted over the ski resort along with showers of black ash, the skifield was closed. But the wind changed direction again, and Mike, the company manager, sent the snow groomers to push the ash off the runs, so we could reopen. It then became necessary to create a symbol for ash on our weather station. Our avalanche forecasting team sorted this for us. It was an upside-down V with three lines coming from the top. The total snowpack was around 3m deep, but it was melting at an impressive speed of 1cm per daylight hour. The usual bright whites of the mountain were being replaced by moody greys and the usual quietness replaced by trickling water.

Skiing on the ash-covered slopes off-piste was like skiing on sand. Our skis left faint white lines over the grey ash and we had to keep our weight way back as gravity made our bodies want to go faster than our skis. You wouldn't call it enjoyable skiing, more survival. But it was fun all the same. It wasn't good for our skis at all. The edges went all rusty and the smooth bases ended up like sandpaper. But how often do you get to ski on a live volcano?

15

A FATAL HELICOPTER CRASH

What I saw out the front window of the helicopter was horrifying. It was 11.07am on 16 August 2014. The snow-covered ground was coming up way too fast, we were going to hit hard and there was nothing I could do. No time to say goodbyes, no life flashing before my eyes. No 'I'm going to die' feeling – just alarm, panic and a sense of acceptance.

'Pull up! Pull up!' I yelled ineffectively at the pilot . . .

I'd had a few near misses in helicopters over the years and they were generally a fun experience, such as jumping out of the moving helicopter when we went to ski Mt D'Archiac. Another time was when a Hughes 500 helicopter turned up to collect four of us from Chancellor Hut on the West Coast. We had huge packs containing bivvy gear, skis and climbing gear. This is a smallish five-person (including the pilot) helicopter, and the helipad at Chancellor is a small grassy knoll, an easy stroll above the hut in a lovely grassy meadow.

I must say that the view from the toilet down the glacier is one of the best toilet views in the world; the grass meadows flow off a cliff to a backdrop of white glacier, green thick bush and further away the deep blue Tasman Sea. But on the other side of the helipad there was a 200m vertical cliff, carved out by the slow-moving Fox Glacier, which had retreated well below its former height and glory. If you dropped a stone from the helipad it would free fall 200m into gaping crevasses in the icefall below.

We had too much gear, so I was sitting in the back on one pack; the seats had been folded up and another pack was wedged between my legs. I was wearing my seatbelt. A friend in the same position sat next to me. Two more were in the front, while the ski gear was in the ski basket on the outside.

'Let's see if we can get off the ground,' said the pilot.

'What could possibly go wrong?' I thought.

With full power on, he slowly lifted the small machine a metre off the ground and tipped it sideways down the 200m cliff, turning it towards the glacier below, which loomed large through the front windscreen. We were flying straight down, but when he had built up enough air speed he lifted the nose and slowly pulled out of the dive. We turned and flew down the glacier to Fox township.

I'm not a pilot, so I had no idea if that was dodgy flying or great flying. But it sure was exciting!

At the same spot a few years later, it was blowing 30 knots and I was waiting for a pickup with four clients. I didn't think the B2 (a bigger helicopter) would land, but he came in, put one skid down and indicated for us to jump in fast. I helped the clients aboard and loaded the gear and was just about to step in when a strong gust hit. The machine was blown off the ground. He pulled up. The helicopter was swinging wildly in the strong winds with its doors open and me holding a handful of gear (nothing useful like a sleeping bag or food). I thought he'd leave me there and I'd be walking the 10 hours down to town, but after a few seconds he came back in and touched down one skid again. I grabbed the hand strap by the door and stood on the skid as once again he was blown off the ridge. I was 200m above the glacier standing on the skid then I climbed into the back seat and pulled the doors closed. We were off down to Fox.

'A bit windy eh!' I said to the pilot. He agreed in his typical, non-dramatic West Coast style.

Heli-skiing is one of the more challenging forms of flying. Machines land on small summits often with limited blade clearance. Some pilots love it and thrive on it, while others stay away.

Helicopters and pilots in New Zealand are surrounded by history and folklore. The boundaries were pushed well beyond safety margins in the 1980s when they were used for deer recovery, and several crashed annually.

I remember the classic story of a company safety officer spotting a pilot fuelling his helicopter while smoking a cigarette. The guy went berserk at the pilot and said you can't do that. The pilot, a fairly stout guy, threw the cigarette on the ground, pulled the fuel nozzle from the helicopter and squirted fuel on the burning cigarette, putting it out. The safety officer walked away shaking his head.

In August 2012 we were heli-skiing near Wanaka. Each day at lunch we'd shut down the helicopter and enjoy an amazing buffet lunch, together with our clients, of hot soup, fresh bread with meat and salads, accompanied by million-dollar views. We'd make a table from snow and cover it with a black tablecloth. It was the most relaxing part of the day because during the rest of it I was always busy looking at the snowpack (checking for avalanche danger), hunting good snow (it's not always easy to find), helping other guides via the radio, talking to the pilot (about fuel requirements and logistics) and giving our clients a good time. Lunch was usually a break and a brief timeout for guides.

I'd flown with this pilot a few times. He wasn't a regular,

although he was a nice guy and an amazing pilot with his own machine. We were skiing a run called Dr Who and there was a well packed-down lunch spot at the foot of the run where groups had been picked up before. I pointed this out as we flew in and asked him to land there and put out the lunch, then he could go and get fuel while we ate – standard practice.

I was skiing the run and he had dropped the other groups above me when I noticed he'd landed 200-300m above the spot we'd discussed. It looked okay from where I was, a kilometre or so up the mountain. Not too steep, in fresh snow, but not somewhere I'd choose personally because it wasn't completely flat. He had already put the lunch bins out and was walking back to the helicopter (which was running), so I couldn't discuss it with him because he wouldn't hear the radio.

As he stood on the step to climb back into the helicopter, his weight caused the helicopter to tip forwards as the snow under the front of the skids collapsed. The blades struck the snow and exploded. My jaw dropped, I was so shocked. I was far enough away that there was almost no sound, but the destruction was instant. In a blink of an eye the helicopter was a right-off. It jerked sideways and threw the pilot backwards off the step into the snow. Initially I was worried that he'd been hurt or killed but he quickly stood up. He told me later he'd felt the air from the exploding rotor blades miss his head by a few centimetres. The helicopter was destroyed.

'We're going to need another helicopter,' I said when I called the guide above me.

A couple of years later, not far away on Mt Alta, a pilot had shut down the helicopter on a nice flat spot part way down a steep run. We flew over them as they ate lunch after we'd skied another run nearby before we went around the corner to the west side of Mt Alta to look at a landing site. I didn't like the look of the regular one. I had snowboarders and it required too much traversing, so I asked Nick, the pilot, to move further back towards the ridge.

The spot I'd chosen wasn't flat enough, so we carried on down the ridge looking at a few other options. We couldn't see the group having lunch on the other side of the ridge.

Nick picked out a good-looking spot between two large rocks and I agreed. However, after he landed and was reducing the power, the snow under us fell away. Nick was an awesome pilot and he anticipated this. I was mostly unaware the snow had dropped as he lifted off to take a look. The snow ridge in front of us fell away as he was lifting.

Through the gap in the ridge I saw the other helicopter, which was shut down on the other side of the mountain.

'That's not good,' said Nick.

'Shit!' I replied.

It should have been far enough away not to be an issue, but when the 5m of cornice landed on the slope below, instead of breaking up and sinking into the snow, which would happen 99 times out of 100, it stayed in one piece and slid on the icy snow surface directly towards the shut-down helicopter. Sadly for the pilot of the other machine, he'd just got back into his helicopter to do something when he saw the massive block of snow sliding towards him. He dived over the back seat as it hit the door frame and bumped the helicopter about a metre. It caused some damage, but it could have been much worse.

It was extra traumatising for him because he'd recently survived a horrific helicopter crash in Papua New Guinea when he was taking out cut trees in the jungle for a forestry operation. He was lifting a tree when his helicopter was suddenly surrounded by cloud and he lost the horizon, which helicopter pilots need to stay upright. Next thing he knew he'd come out of the cloud going sideways and downwards into the jungle. His helicopter crashed into the tall trees and was destroyed as the blades flew off.

Luckily the log he was lifting caught in the branches and the cable hung over a higher tree. His machine ended up hanging upside down in the thick jungle from the steel cable only a metre off the ground. He undid his seatbelt and stepped from the helicopter onto the ground.

Sadly, Nick was killed in 2018, when the door of his helicopter sprung open and sucked out some overalls, which hit the tail rotor, causing the entire tail boom to come off. It would have been impossible to control the helicopter after such catastrophic damage.

Back to 2014. I'd been working for Harris Mountains Heli-Ski for around 14 years and the year before had been promoted to chief guide. The chief guide is responsible for all guiding in the field. It was a good job, but also a tough one. I was required to exert control over, or more accurately 'shepherd', many of my best friends, who were all super-experienced guides and mostly older than me. I got the job partly because no one else wanted it, but also because I was the most qualified and suitably experienced. I enjoyed mentoring guides and I was very active in the guiding industry. A number of our team could do it, but few wanted the responsibility or the headaches. I often referred to the role as 'the herder of cats'.

I'd ask Whitney, one of the guides, where he'd skied that day, to check in and see if there were any problems.

He'd say, 'Arrrh, you wouldn't know the run, you're too young.'

My usual reply was to ask, 'Are you so old you've forgotten?'

It wasn't an easy job!

During guide training that year I'd had a heated discussion with another senior guide, a past chief guide and a friend. He insisted that our helicopter supplier introduced a weight-and-balance procedure. He'd worked in Alaska where it was common practice. I'd only heard of it in Alaska, and said we'd look into it. A weight-and-balance calculation is when clients, guides, ski gear, lunch and fuel are all measured and calculated to ensure that the helicopter is within its weight limits and that the weight is balanced around the centre of the rotor blades. Until then I thought it was done by the pilots eyeballing the people.

When Roger and I raised it with THL, the helicopter company that owned us, we were initially met with a little scepticism.

But the company management bought into it and introduced a declared-weight system. We would add 4kg to account for clothes, since most people weigh themselves naked. Apparently this was an approved system for accurately measuring the internal weight of a helicopter. I was not aware of any other company in New Zealand weighing people. We also added 7kg for skis and 5kg for snowboards.

Working out load sheets covering people, their abilities and how many runs they wanted to do was done the night before. It was a complicated procedure and was done very old school with pencils and rubbers. We had just started to add the declared weights to the load sheets. The completed load sheets were then faxed to Queenstown to the pilots, who had the final say over the weight and balance. Guides were considered a passenger and a loader.

The next day started normally enough. I was at Harris Mountains operations room at 7am as usual, looking at the weather and the day's planning from the night before. Five helicopters were working with about 12 loads of five heli-ski clients and a guide. We had our morning meeting, connected to the Queenstown guides via Skype, and discussed avalanche danger, logistics and other dangers we needed to manage that day. The snow wasn't great – wind-packed hard snow and not what the typical heli-ski client is expecting. The skiing would not be that good.

I reminded the guides that the day was going to be about good guiding and entertaining our clients to make their experience a *once in a lifetime* event. It is classic how one guide can reach the bottom of a run and not say much, look a bit bored and appear not to be enjoying themselves. Then the bottom of the same run with another guide who is obviously having fun, pointing out mountains, telling them how good their turn was, or complimenting them on their nice skis. One group of clients will be having a ball. The others may want their money back.

Our team was highly experienced. At 44 I was one of the young ones and I still got ribbed by guides with 20 to 25 years' experience. It was a good-fun group to work with. They were some of the best in the industry and their skills and qualities were world class. Many of our pilots were also world class.

My group of five would be flying over from Queenstown, so my morning was somewhat relaxed. I was the lead guide for the helicopter and there were two other guides assisting me with five clients each. While we were skiing, the pilot would move the other groups up the mountains, where we would regroup around lunchtime for a picnic somewhere in the snow.

I had worked with Dave the pilot many times before and usually enjoyed it. A few of the other guides didn't like working with Dave. He was slow flying from A to B. But I was happy with him. I felt he was just being cautious and there was nothing wrong with being a little slow to fly, especially to land. He would come into a landing quite high, then move directly downwards from around 20 to 50m above as he lined up the landing spot. There were a couple of other pilots who flew this way, but most flew in briskly and confidently just below the landing height and came upwards, flaring and slowing quickly before settling down softly on the landing spot.

I'd had a mild warning about Dave the week before. I'd mucked up my ski line and gone too low into steep terrain. I found a small ridge for Dave to land one skid on while we climbed in. It was a tough situation for a pilot and I'd told Dave to say so if he wasn't happy. He said we'd give it a crack. I loaded in the guests while Dave hovered with one skid on the small ridge; the other one was in open space. While this sounds quite dramatic, it isn't too serious and in somewhere like Alaska is very common practice.

I briefed the clients about climbing in softly and slowly. 'Treat it like stepping onto a small dinghy,' I said, which they did. They secured their seatbelts once they were in.

Then without warning Dave lifted off, with all the doors open and the other guide Chris still halfway through loading the skis. I was half in the front seat and quickly put the headset on to tell Dave to go back down, because we were only halfway through packing the skis into the basket. Luckily Chris hadn't been knocked off when Dave lifted off. Dave put the skid back on the ridge and Chris loaded the rest of the gear, closed the basket and climbed in. We looked at each other and shook our heads as we gave each other a knowing smile.

Later we agreed how weird that had been.

Chris said to me, 'What was he thinking?'

But I blamed myself for putting the pilot in a difficult situation. I'd skied too low and chosen a poor pickup. We should have taken off our skis and hiked for ten minutes to a better spot. Chris was more adamant that it should have been easy for the pilot.

I had chosen a poor run a few years earlier, as guides occasionally do. I skied down the wrong line and it got steeper and steeper. By then we were committed. It turned into a steep chute with rocks either side. I could ski it fine, small jump turns from side to side. But the clients all simultaneously fell over, rolling down the snow harmlessly and losing their skis on the way. Because the snow was soft they didn't pick up speed but just bumped their way down between the rocks of the steep couloir.

We gathered at the bottom, everyone with smiles on their faces and laughing. No harm done. I hiked back up and collected their equipment. Funnily enough they all enjoyed the experience. I probably could have kept it quiet if it hadn't been for the other groups having lunch below us. They called me Tumble Weed for a while after that.

Back to 16 August. When I met Dave to discuss the day he mentioned that the clients were a little heavy, but he said it wasn't a problem, he'd manage it. The helicopter safety briefing was carried out by Mike, another guide in Queenstown, before they'd flown over. Then I ran through the avalanche safety briefing with the clients and we loaded the helicopter to fly in for the first run.

We headed into the Triple Peak area to a run called Tony's Ridge. It's a nice easy run to start on and about halfway down it steepens into a nice east-facing slope, which I predicted would have softened in the morning sunshine.

I was a little taken aback when during the flight in Dave turned to me.

'I'll sneak on some extra fuel so that I won't need to fly out to refuel during the day.'

I imagined he was thinking he'd save helicopter time and make the company more money.

'Please don't,' I said. 'It's no problem to get fuel. Plus it's not our money. Let's just make it easy on ourselves.'

I didn't want him to overload the helicopter just to save money! He nodded.

Taking on extra fuel would make the load even heavier than it already was. I never did ask him if he actually took on that extra fuel. I suspect he didn't, but I fear he might have. I trusted him and didn't think about it again until the investigation later.

We landed at the top of the run and the group were excited when the helicopter left. We could see Aoraki/Mt Cook to the north, Tititea/Mt Aspiring to the west and a lifetime's worth of ski lines and mountains all around us. I explained how to ski the terrain safely because hazards weren't marked – always stop above me, ski in control, all the usual stuff. Then we were off down the wind-packed powder. The snow was what I'd call average, but the guys loved it and were hooting and hollering as they snowboarded and skied the untracked snow. We stopped for a rest and then took on the next slope below.

Jerome, one of the clients, had brought his camera fitted with a big 200mm lens and I set up the guys so he could snap some photos. When the snow changed to spring corn as I'd expected we skied a steep chute down to the river and our pickup spot. 'Corn' is when the sun softens the frozen snow; it is very easy and fun to ski on.

While we waited, the next group skied a steeper line. They were a Red Bull film crew and they leapt off a large rock, much to our amazement. 'If only we were younger,' one of the guys said.

The helicopter swooped in to pick us up and we flew to Mt Alta. When we lifted off I noticed that Dave didn't lift up very high from the ground before he slowly turned the machine to face down the slope. He then tipped the helicopter forward, slowly building up airspeed quite close to the snow before he lifted higher away from the ground. I assumed it was because he had taken on the maximum weight of fuel in relation to our internal weight. All pretty normal stuff.

I asked him to fly past the south face of Mt Alta so I could check the snow. It looked good, and we carried on around to the east face. I pointed out an easier ski line for the third group of skiers, who were a lower skill level. We headed to the north-west shoulder, a common landing site.

Initially we flew over it to check for wind and look for the landing flag, but we couldn't spot it so Dave banked a turn back towards the landing, much to everybody's enjoyment. They cheered loudly from the back seats. I smiled. The guys were having fun.

We flew into the landing from the south and spotted the flag, blowing gently and indicating a south-west breeze. It had blown over and was lying almost horizontal. Still the flag indicated a light southerly. Dave flew past again and banked to the right and lined up the landing.

We were coming in slowly and although I was looking down the slope below at a ski line, it felt as if everything was normal.

Until Dave shouted, 'No,' and turned hard to the left. We started sinking.

One theory about what happened was that we got caught in a vortex ring. This is when the pilot descends at the wrong speed and the air from the rotors is recirculated back into the blades, causing the helicopter to fall from the sky. Vortex ring conditions occur during approaches with a tailwind. It's likely we did experience a tail wind because a thermal breeze was coming up the north face of Mt Alta.

I came to the conclusion, almost a year later, after talking to other pilots and even landing there several times in the same conditions, that we'd flown into a corner, so when he aborted the landing (which happens sometimes) there was no room to turn before the mountain. He'd had to bank steeply, which in turn caused the helicopter to lose airspeed. Then he'd had to dip the helicopter down to fly forward, to build up the airspeed that would allow him to fly away. Only there was a snow slope below.

That was when I saw the snow-covered ground coming up way too fast. We were going to hit hard and there was nothing I could do.

The impact was harder and more violent than anything I had ever experienced. I felt us smash into the snow with so much force I felt like I was being crushed flat. Then we exploded upwards as my world went dark, most likely because I closed my eyes.

I was tossed downward in circles. I couldn't tell if I was in the helicopter or out of it. There was violent thrashing about and forces on my body that I didn't think were survivable. I could hear a deafening screeching of metals being torn apart. I felt entirely alone, my world was reduced to sound and pain. I couldn't hear anyone else.

Then I was being driven headfirst through the snow at high speed. I was definitely out of the helicopter by then and had no control at all. I started a high speed tomahawk, tumbling head to foot, head to foot, head to foot, thumping loudly with each hit on the snow, for what I later estimated to be 100m.

Finally I slowed down and came to rest on my hands and knees. Silence. Not breathing. Pain.

The world was half dark and I couldn't breathe. One eye was swollen shut and I was badly winded.

After what seemed like an eternity I took a few breaths and smelt the cloying stench of aviation fuel. I spat out what I thought was food and briefly wondered what I had been eating before I realised it was bits of teeth.

I forced my other eye open to check where the rest of the helicopter was – I was worried about fire. But it was nowhere to be seen.

I still wasn't breathing properly, but as I took shallow breaths and opened one eye I turned my radio to the repeater channel to raise the alarm. I couldn't reach our base via the repeater as I was below the ridge, so I changed it back to simplex (line of sight). Through gasping breaths I called Mike and Katie, the other two guides who were working with me.

'Mayday, Mayday, we have crashed our helicopter, multiple

casualties, helicopter is destroyed, stop all heli-skiing and get everyone here to help. Call the Search and Rescue, police, paramedics, bring all our rescue gear. This is a major incident.'

It was then that I spotted one of the clients near me, in a stupor and obviously in shock. He was bleeding from a head wound and holding his arm. I could only talk in a whisper and I thought my lung must have collapsed when I landed on my radio.

There was another person just above us. He'd landed next to the first aid kit and the shovel. He sat on the shovel, grabbed the first aid kit and slid down the snow to us and asked what he should do. 'Can you bandage his head?' I whispered.

When I looked down, the pilot was about 70m below us. His head was bloody. He was trying to climb up to us, but he was staggering about in circles instead.

I checked in with Katie via the radio to ensure the word was out, then the guy who was okay asked, 'What should I do now?'

We agreed that the guy with the broken arm could watch me while the other two went down to the wreckage and checked on the remaining passengers. Some days later he found out that he had an unstable fractured vertebra and could have severed his spinal cord with one wrong move.

Then there was me – I was still struggling to breathe.

An eternity later, although probably only 15 minutes, I heard the welcome sound of a helicopter approaching. It landed without any trouble at the top of our run where we had intended to land. Within a short time my good friend Whitney was standing over me laughing.

'You're alive!' he said. Apparently from the look of the wreckage, he wasn't expecting to see any survivors.

I replied, 'I'm having trouble breathing,' and his smile turned to concern. He later said he could barely recognise me – swollen face, closed eye and bruising.

Whitney made me more comfortable and made sure oxygen was on its way. The other guide who'd come in, Mike, called up to say four were okay, but one was deceased.

Whitney shovelled out a flat spot in the snow for me to lie on.

I was lying half on my side, with my chest on his guide pack, but everything hurt. I pushed the concerns about my lung out of my head because I knew that wouldn't help me right now (a punctured lung can cause a tension pneumothorax, and that lung can quickly collapse).

It was almost an hour after the crash when I was finally hooked up to oxygen, and after another hour I'd had a shot of morphine and a spinal check. It was the most uncomfortable two hours of my life. My ribs and back were excruciating. I was having trouble breathing. I was so cold from lying on the snow I was shivering uncontrollably, causing the ends of my rib fractures to rub together.

Eventually I was winched off the site with the onset of hypothermia, screaming out in pain because the harness they put me in was crushing my ribs. When the rescuers got me level with the helicopter door they reached out and roughly dragged me inside the helicopter with no care for my fractures and I screamed again.

We landed at a staging area and I was half carried, half dragged, still screaming in pain, to another helicopter. I was roughly pushed aboard and we took off towards the Wanaka Medical Centre. I was surprised at the panic in the rescuers' eyes and the lack of a backboard, something we always train with for moving someone with such injuries. But I was also very glad to be off the mountain and flying towards the Medical Centre.

I was lying on the floor of the helicopter, which my good friend James was flying. I remember how grim he looked as I watched him through my one open eye. I didn't have a headset and I couldn't talk to him, so I motioned to the paramedic in the back to lean towards me. With a painful smile I asked him to tell James he was a 'homo'. He looked at me shocked and asked me to repeat myself, which I did.

'No way,' he said. I relaxed on the floor. Apparently he got up the nerve to tell James, a real West Coaster, what I'd said later on that day. It made him laugh, and it was then that he realised I'd be okay. Needless to say, I have nothing against gay people!

After landing at the clinic, I was put on a stretcher. I had my boots removed and they covered me with blankets. Jo came to see me before they whisked me away in another helicopter to Dunedin hospital for x-rays and CT scans. By midnight I was heavily sedated in a warm bed with four broken ribs (on three different sides), one compression fracture of my lumbar spine, two vertebrae fractures (the transverse processes), five stitches, chipped teeth and a laceration to my skull, while my chin was super-glued together and that's without mentioning several haematomas and abrasions – I was black and blue.

What saved me? Luck, luck and more luck. The forces on my body tore the seatbelt off the floor and I was ejected out of the helicopter. My eyes were closed, but I felt as if I went out through the small window space by my feet. We hit snow and not rocks (they were 5m to the left and right); there was a quick rescue; and more luck! If you re-ran that accident 1000 times, 999 times everyone would die instantly.

One passenger was uninjured; three had minor head injuries and two had broken backs, another a broken arm. Then there were Jerome's fatal injuries. Jerome was a client from Auckland whom I didn't know. He left behind a family – a son and a wife. Six of us were incredibly lucky, but our thoughts were with Jerome's family and friends. Really, all of us should have died. I think we hit the ground at speeds of 75-100 km/hr.

I spent two nights in hospital then Jo took me home. The pain continued to be unbearable and for weeks I could barely move. It was a combination of the back and rib fractures on different sides of my torso. There was no position to sit without pain and moving was excruciating. I took the maximum dosage of the opiate pain relief called Tramadol. I was terrified of sneezing or getting a cold or a cough. The first day home I tried to walk down my street and managed only 100m at a slow shuffle before I had to go home.

Jo was ever the patient nurse and it can't have been easy treating me while I was in so much pain. When treating someone you know and love you seem to share their pain. The Tramadol blocked up my bowels and it was a week before I got the right balance of laxatives to pass a bowel movement.

For the first week I had to sleep on a mattress on the floor because our bed was too soft. Eventually I made it to bed, but I had to wake up every few hours to take pain relief. I'd roll onto my side and ever so painfully get out of bed. Jo let me use my mountaineering pee bottle, which really helped. While taking a pee I could lie on my back and not move. That old mountaineering trick came in handy.

The accident was the start of a four-week period of fine weather. It was hard to be cooped up all day. I had a lot of visitors and each one seemed to receive a shock when they saw how bad I looked and how much pain I was in. I felt lucky, but also quite down. What helped was short walks each day as I slowly built up distance, regaining my strength.

Once again ACC came to the party. They gave me an electric La-Z-Boy chair, which enabled me to back into it in a standing position, then lean against it and push the button, so it slowly took me into a sitting position. Getting up or sitting down normally was the most painful movement.

The crash investigation went on for seven years. It was a pathetically slow process and I imagined how hard the investigation must have been on Jerome's family. Surely they needed an explanation of what had gone wrong. Because of the ongoing investigation I wasn't allowed to communicate with them or comment.

Several theories were thrown about and finally the Civil Aviation Authority investigation announced that the helicopter was overloaded by 20kg, which was insane. There was no way that caused the accident – 20kg on top of a 1200kg helicopter with 400kg of fuel and seven people averaging 90kg each.

The coroner said the pilot did not comply with the pre-flight procedure in that he used declared weights to calculate the weight and balance of the helicopter but did not add the mandatory 4kg for each declared weight. Had he done so, the internal load before fuel would have been 2270kg (as opposed to the maximum permissible internal weight of 2250kg). I just don't accept this was the cause of the accident.

Dave was being as careful as he could be, but maybe he chose the wrong approach path? He wasn't a rookie or a cowboy. He had meticulously checked everything.

At the end of the day I believe it was just an accident, similar to driving your car too fast around a corner on a winter night and hitting ice or gravel, which causes your car to slide sideways and hit the only tree in sight, right on the passenger door next to where someone is sitting. Everyone in the car would be lucky to survive, because if you hadn't hit that tree there was a 200m cliff down below to the ocean.

After three months in a Tramadol daze, the pain relented enough for me to give it up. But by then my body had become addicted to it. When I stopped taking it, I started sweating and shaking. I went to the doctor and he prescribed Valium. After a day of that I woke up feeling as if a fog had been lifted from my brain. I didn't realise how bad the Tramadol was making me feel both night and day.

A year later every person and every piece of gear was meticulously weighed. We almost never take a client in the front seat (only four clients in the back seat). And I saw how differently the pilots flew with lighter loads. My accident increased safety for sure and I continue to enjoy heli-skiing in New Zealand.

I often get asked, 'How do you feel getting back in a helicopter?' My usual reply is, 'If we crash, we are all going to die.'

There is no point worrying about it. I accept that risk before setting off for the day, and if a pilot is having an off day, the weather isn't right, or I feel something isn't right, I'll call off the day and fly back to the valley. No second thoughts. If you fly in a helicopter you just have to accept that it might well crash. Same with getting in a car or a boat, nothing is guaranteed.

I carried on at rehab with my usual feverish enthusiasm and within five months I was back leading an expedition to guide five people to Mt Vinson, the highest peak in Antarctica.

Above: Heading off for a tramp on Great Barrier Island at age 15.

Right: Fence jumping in Austria.

Below: Ski bums in 1992 living by the train tracks near Mt Ruapehu.

Above: Skiing ash-covered Mt Ruapehu.

Below: Mt Ruapehu erupts, x marks the spot where Mark was standing when this photo was taken.

Above left: Climbing what was at the time NZ's hardest ice climb, the Balfour Face of Mt Tasman.

Above right: Mark on the cover of NZ Skier Magazine in 1997.

Below: Day 4 of 5 on The Shield, El Capitan, Yosemite Valley, USA.

Above: The impressive Ama Dablam in the Nepal Himalaya. Site of the Sherpa rescue.

Bottom: Mark landed his paraglider in a remote village in Tanzania and was rather popular! Five minutes before the field was empty.

Top: Mt Green in summer where Mark got avalanched in 1995. You can't see the crevasses in winter, but x marks the burial spot.

Centre: Life in the snow cave.

Right: Buried alive in a large crevasse. The main crevasse is to the left.

Above: Mt Everest's South Summit.

Below: Mark on the summit, May 21, 2007.

Kids of the Khumbu, Mark loved to photograph the local children.

Above: Happy wife, happy life, Jo in Antarctica snowboarding with penguins.

Right: Mark on deck helping cut away the jib sail while in 15 metre swells crossing the Drake Passage towards Cape Horn from Antarctica.

Above left: The shipping container we spent 5 days in.

Above: Starved and trapped, inside the shipping container.

Below: The Tyrollean Traverse high on Carstensz Pyramid, Papua, Eastern Indonesia.

Kite skiing towards The Spectre.

Climbing The Spectre.

-60 C near the South Pole.

Spectre summit.

Outer worldly.

Christmas near the South Pole.

The pulk in the crevasse.

A rest out of the wind dressed for -60 C.

A 22° halo with double sun dogs, a sun pillar and a parhelic circle near the South Pole.

Above: Mt Alta helicopter crash site with Mark being treated.

Left: Mt Alta crash site.

Below: Mark battered, broken, swollen and bruised.

16

IS MY BRAIN EXPLODING?

Few activities can emulate the feeling of powder skiing, but kitesurfing is one that comes close. Harnessing the wind creates the feeling of gravity found in skiing. The pull of the wind can even be greater than the pull of gravity. The kite also adds to the weightless feeling of skiing, dragging me across the silky-smooth face of a wave, until the wave rises and takes over. It pushes me along on my surfboard, propelling me forward until I lean over and turn the board back up towards the lip of the wave while the kite waits patiently for a request for power. But for now, thanks to the wave, I don't need it and I glance up at the lip of the wave, sometimes 2-3m above me, looming like a moonlit monolith while I finish the turn and head back up towards it. The wave pauses for just a split second while I sneak ahead, then crashes down behind me.

It's another feeling very difficult to explain in words. The feeling of weightlessness, of effortless movement, the euphoria, the sheer joy it brings. Sharing it with friends brings a feeling of joy and happiness, not adrenaline filled but more of a calm satisfaction. Sometimes when I return to the beach after riding a kilometre-long wave, kite landed on the beach, surfboard under my arm, I just sit there for a minute. I'm completely satisfied, exhausted and exhilarated and just soaking in the moment.

I'd first seen kitesurfing in 2002 at Lake Hawea when Dave Hiddleston launched his kite into a stormy strong north-west wind. He had me hold the back of his harness, just next to where his large dive knife was strapped on (in case he needed to cut the kite away) and drag him down to the water's edge, his feet often off the ground from the upward pull of the kite. It was the very early days of kitesurfing, before many of the safety features of today's kites were invented. But seeing Dave drove Jo and I to have some lessons.

We loved it and bought our gear. Finding the right wind back then was difficult, the kites had a small usable range of wind speeds. I'd never been much of a beach dweller. There's nothing to do there. So this gave me an excuse to visit warm places. We did a road trip to Cairns in Australia, rented camper vans and cruised around the coast.

The next place to visit was Vietnam. Jo and I booked a nice hotel right on the beach and kited every day it was windy. One day we rented a scooter and drove 40 minutes north to another beach. Halfway there, in the middle of nowhere, I had to stop with a flat tyre. Within a few minutes we were surrounded by five friendly locals. They detached the wheel and with me holding it and riding on the back of one of their bikes, we took off back down the road to a puncture-repair place. The locals were so friendly they wouldn't even let me pay for the repair. An hour later I got dropped back to Jo with the fixed tyre.

When we approached Jo I smiled broadly. She was surrounded by around 20 children, all smiling and practising their basic English. What is your name, where are you from, etc? They were all laughing and having a great time. With the tyre back on the scooter we carried on our way and kitesurfed a remote beach. These are the sort of adventures kitesurfing would often take you on.

In 2006 I started to ride a surfboard with my kite. I tried it out during a kitesurfing trip to Hawaii where kitesurfing had started.

Then a client whom I guided up Mt Everest had a brother who owned a kite company who sent me a surfboard as a tip after the expedition. Everyone else I knew still rode twin tips (like a wake board), but I worked on mastering the surfboard, which wasn't easy without the foot straps on a twin tip. It took some time.

In 2011 I was kitesurfing in Bali after climbing Carstensz Pyramid. I rented a surfboard and got chatting to the owner of the kite shop. He'd heard of a good spot in Peru where windsurfers had been going for years which he thought might work with a kite. After I got home I researched the spot and it looked great. Jo, Whitney, Kirsten and I set off to Peru in search of waves and wind.

In those days, kitesurfing in cross-offshore winds was unheard of. Everyone either kited in onshore or cross-shore winds. But we managed some great kiting and by the end of the trip we all had surfboards. It was at a remote fishing village in northern Peru, where no one spoke English. I've been going back there for 10 years now, returning for four to five weeks each time, and it remains one of the best spots on the planet to kite. The staff at the hotel we stay in are like family and we have free rein of the place, to make coffee in the kitchen, or wander around on the roof looking at the waves and the wind. No one speaks English and I enjoy learning Spanish and practising it on the locals.

Ten years of travelling to Peru to kitesurf has created some funny memories. Like kiting at a remote beach when a shady-looking car with tinted windows drove across the desert slowly towards us. Our local friend suggested we were about to get robbed at gunpoint and we should all go out on the water kitesurfing. If they stopped we should come ashore and give them whatever they wanted. We quickly hid our passports and wallets in the sand dunes and went out on the water. As the car pulled to a stop next to ours, I reluctantly kited ashore to take what was coming to us. The plan was that the girls could stay safe kiting.

I was walking up the beach towards the dodgy-looking car with a sinking feeling when all four doors opened at once. Out came a young family with two young kids! We instantly started laughing and giving the local guide a ribbing for winding us up.

One day Richard was kiting a couple of kilometres from the shore in light winds near another remote village. The wind died and he ended up floating in the ocean. Two men in a small fishing boat pulled up and he crawled aboard thinking rescue had arrived. The 3m boat floor was covered in strong-smelling fish. In very poor Spanish he suggested they take him ashore for a reward, but they simply shook their heads and pointed towards the beach. Richard reluctantly took a plastic bag from the fishermen, emptied out the fish and stuffed his kite inside, tied the bag closed and threw it in the ocean. He dived in behind it and paddled his surfboard while pushing his kite. Once he got to the waves he was thrown up onto the beach, stinking of fish and exhausted, only to have to catch a motor taxi along the Trans American Highway back to his hotel. He never did get the fish smell out of his kite.

Later we bought a section on the southern coast of New Zealand at a beach called Colac Bay just west of Riverton. It had a small low-roofed shed on it, which we camped in. We installed solar lights and a small pot-belly stove and dug a long-drop toilet. It was our escape from the Wanaka heat and crowds. The trees all grow at a 45° angle on the south coast of the South Island because of the blustery and frequent westerly winds. It's not that dissimilar to Patagonia in South America. And when you live in the mountains it is always enjoyable to escape to the coast with the smell of the sea, the taste of the air, surfing and kitesurfing and living off the grid.

In late summer in 2013 I was a week from leaving for Nepal to set up an Adventure Consultants Everest expedition. I loved the work in Nepal. It was an awesome place to do business, which often involved trekking around the Khumbu Valley, with a backpack full to the brim with Nepali rupees and American dollars.

Back at Colac Bay the waves were huge – their faces were triple my height at around 6m. The wind was extremely gusty, blowing at 40-45 knots. Four of us were kitesurfing the big waves, which were so big that you couldn't ride up the faces once they started breaking – you had to sheet in your kite and jump them. Your timing had to be perfect. For that reason, I had put my foot straps back on my surfboard (I didn't usually use them). The guys I was kiting with – Cookie, Tim and Simon – were all very good kiters, but one by one they were being slammed by the waves and washed ashore in a tangle.

I thought I'd go out and catch one more wave. As I approached a massive breaking one I went to jump, but a strong gust hit me. I was dragged forward as the wave broke on me, hitting my legs and snapping my right leg forcefully backwards. I heard a pop and instantly thought I'd fractured my femur. I was thrown about by the wave, lost my board but kept my kite in the sky. This enabled me to use the kite to drag myself ashore. Lying on my side, I dragged myself up the beach to safety.

Jo caught my kite, but it was then that I realised I'd done something serious to my knee. Back at our shack a doctor friend came to visit and after some pulling and twisting said I'd most likely ruptured my anterior cruciate ligament (ACL). The Nepal trip was off as I concentrated on my rehab programme. I spent hours on the phone and finally found a specialist in Auckland who could see me the following week.

I was already having physiotherapy and doing everything else possible to get back to work as soon as possible. That was music to ACC's ears. They approved everything I'd booked and fully supported me through six months of rehab. Three weeks after the accident I was put under a general anaesthetic for a hamstring graft ACL replacement. People love to put down New Zealand's medical system, but if you have hurt yourself from an obvious accident, ACC is an amazing system and it worked like a charm for my injury.

After the operation I became obsessed with rehab. I swam, biked, worked out at the gym and even had a personal trainer (thanks to ACC). On average I'd be in the gym five hours a day. I ate fish oil and anything else that the internet told me would help speed up my recovery.

I started kitesurfing again gently after six or seven months wearing a knee brace. After eight or nine months I was out kiting when I realised my knee brace was on the wrong leg. I laughed aloud and decided at that point that my knee was well and truly fixed.

That was the second injury requiring hospitalisation while I was in my forties, but there was worse.

In 2009 I led my first unsuccessful expedition. It was on Mt Cho Oyu in Tibet, the fifth highest mountain in the world and one of the 8000m peaks. We started late in the season because the Chinese had closed it and we were planning an alternative climb of an 8000m peak in Nepal. But then they opened it at the last minute and since it was an easier mountain, we changed our destination.

Unfortunately when the jet stream arrived early, there was no way to get to the summit. The jet stream is a band of gale-force winds that flow around the globe at around 8000m and move north during the regular mountaineer season. We had climbed to just under 7000m and had to abandon the expedition. That meant I had spare time in Nepal, so I went down to Pokhara and took private instruction in paragliding. I'd been flying for a few years, mostly teaching myself after an initial two-day course. I'd taken my lightweight wing to Everest Base Camp and hiked and flown some small hills on the way (all over 5000m). It was a good way to build on my skills and obtain the next level of certificate so I could legally fly on my own in New Zealand.

I arrived home in November, and Jo and I took off to the South Coast.

On this particular day I was pumping up my kite to head into the waves when it felt as if a paintball (a game where players shoot each other with balls of coloured dye) had exploded inside my head. The pain was immense. I screamed and clutched at my head.

'Something is wrong with my head. You have to take me to hospital, now!' I shouted to Jo, who was sheltering from the wind in the car.

She packed away my kite and rushed me to the nearest medical clinic 10 minutes away in Riverton. The last thing I remember was dashing into the clinic behind her and blacking out.

I'd had a subarachnoid haemorrhage (SAH), which is a type of brain aneurysm that can kill you. It's a form of stroke caused by bleeding into the space surrounding the brain. SAHs occurs in about one per 10,000 people. Older females who smoke are more commonly affected. There's a 30-45% chance they'll be fatal. I can only imagine what would have happened if this had occurred while I was in the Himalayas the week before. I would, most certainly, have died.

Apparently the clinic gave me morphine for the pain, then put me in an ambulance bound for Invercargill, an hour's drive away. They carried out scans and then flew me to Christchurch Hospital, where the South Island's top neurologists work. When I stopped responding to any stimuli that evening, they operated and drilled a hole in the top of my head to insert a drain which relieved the pressure. I don't remember much, but I do remember being confused about why everyone at the dance party was dressed as nurses and why I couldn't leave and go home with Jo.

They prepped me for another operation where they intended to go in through the femoral artery in my groin and follow it up to my brain, where they would put a coil around the ruptured blood vessel. But after several scans they couldn't isolate the bleed and as my condition improved, I avoided the operation.

After I'd been a week in bed a nurse told me I was to get a sponge bath. It was the best news I'd had in days and images of a cute young nurse with a soft sponge covered in soap foam quickly entered my mind. That vision vanished relatively fast as a large Samoan man entered the room with a bucket of water and wearing thick yellow gloves.

Two weeks later I was discharged from hospital. Recovery from an SAH is the same as for many head injuries – slow and unknown. When I left the hospital I walked 100m, then slept for four hours. It was six months before I was fully recovered.

The doctor's advice was to carry on climbing any mountains that I wanted to but to stay away from alcohol for six months. I was interested when he said in my final exam that smoking pot and taking ecstasy or LSD were all fine, but never to touch cocaine or speed. I wasn't sure what to make of his comments. From the USA, he was obviously a free-thinking brain surgeon. I asked him if the high altitude might have caused it and he said a definitive 'No'.

Experiencing a medical issue makes you feel very mortal. It doesn't matter how bullet proof, fit and healthy you are, the cold-steel syringes in hospital hands push through the toughest defences.

After I was diagnosed with an elevated prostate specific antigen (PSA) level, my doctor sent me for a biopsy. He made a humorously inappropriate suggestion that I choose a specialist with small fingers. Call it inappropriate or just good advice; you actually don't have much choice.

I lay on my side in preparation for the examination. A quick check and out came the cold steel instrument to take the biopsy. I was too afraid to look over my shoulder in case it was the size of a large bolt cutter. The pain of the snip brought tears to my eyes, and then he told me he'd missed. Three more tries, many tears and groaning and it was finally done.

I was given antibiotics because apparently one in 300 men get an infection. It was heli-ski season, and the next morning I went to work but I was feeling a little weird and shaky. The weather was bad, so the trip was cancelled. I went home to rest. A few hours later, I was sweating and feeling as if I had the flu. I knew it was a sign of infection.

It was the weekend, so I went to see the on-call doctor, who thought I was fine, but she insisted on calling the doctor who had taken the biopsy. He couldn't be reached, but his assistant said I needed to go to the hospital immediately. I called Jo, who was snowboarding at Treble Cone, and asked her to drive me. I went home to pack and it was then that the specialist called and insisted I go by *ambulance* to hospital.

Ten to 15 minutes after arriving at the hospital, which was an hour's drive away, I had an uncontrollable fever and I was admitted to the Intensive Care Unit with chronic septicemia. Later that night, I ripped off my hospital gown and was found trying to escape through a locked door. I was delirious and near death with a 43°C temperature. They restrained me and finally found the right antibiotic to get the infection under control.

Over the next 24 hours my temperature dropped and I was eventually discharged. The biopsy came back with no signs of cancer and it turned out I had nothing more than an over-active prostate, which gives a high PSA reading.

17

BLOWING STUFF UP

I was tied in place, my backside perched on the floor of a helicopter loaded with explosives, my legs hanging out where the door would usually be, flying high over a dangerous avalanche slope on a cool winter morning in Wanaka. I lit the 90-second fuse and checked for ignition – it was burning.

As I threw the heavy bomb over the side, a violent gust of wind tipped the helicopter sideways and I didn't throw it properly. The 15kg bomb landed on the skid of the helicopter and I pretty much choked in shock . . .

I think my fascination with explosives started when I was young during the annual Guy Fawkes celebrations. We'd buy as many firecrackers as we could afford and cause havoc around the neighbourhood.

In 1993 I got my explosives licence for avalanche control after a two-day course which culminated in blowing up old tree stumps. I was in heaven.

I'd taken on a job ski patrolling at Turoa and I just loved the avalanche control work. We'd make up bombs in old 2-litre plastic milk bottles by filling them with ANFO and tossing them on the dangerous slopes, so that when they exploded they'd set off an avalanche.

The search and rescue training day planned for the local avalanche rescue-team members involved the police, their search dogs, the Department of Conservation staff and ski patrol members. We wanted to run the scenario in natural avalanche debris on a path called the Black & White Couloir and I was sent down with bombs to start an avalanche. It was during a storm with white-out conditions and strong winds. I bumped into Dave, a Department of Conservation worker from Whakapapa, who had an avalanche victim dummy in overalls stuffed with foam with him. It was his pride and joy and he wanted me to dig it into the avalanche debris and see if the police dogs could find it.

As I skied towards the scenario I came up with a better idea. I threw the dummy over the cornice into the Black & White Couloir and got a bomb ready. I would set the avalanche off so that it travelled down and buried Dave's dummy naturally. Visibility was down below a few metres as I tossed the bomb over the cornice and down the slope out of sight. Bombs are tied to a rope so that they don't bounce down the slope, because they won't achieve anything if they explode at the bottom. I sat there holding the bomb rope waiting for the explosion.

As I expected, it came 90 seconds later and because the wind was blowing up the slope, I was expecting snow to fly over the cornice. Instead I was horrified to see hundreds of pieces of Dave's dummy mixed in with the snow. The dummy hadn't slid down the slope and my bomb had landed directly on it. The resulting avalanche debris were mixed up with pieces of Dave's dummy. The police dogs searched for a few seconds then one of them picked up a piece of the dummy in its teeth. Dave was angry with me and although most of the others saw the funny side, he did not. It was some years later before we could laugh about it together.

Others who don't find explosives funny are security personnel at airports. One year I had been doing avalanche control work on the morning I flew out of Utah at the end of winter; this was pre the 9/11 terror attacks in America. Security agents swabbed my backpack and put the samples in the testing machine. I never thought much about it, but several alarms with flashing lights went off and within an instant I was surrounded by heavily armed police. They emptied my pack and some pink pieces of ANFO explosives fell out onto the table. I explained my job and what I had been doing, and after some thought they let me carry on and board the plane.

Note: A climax avalanche is when an entire slope avalanches, including all the layers. All that is left is the ground.

It was 29 January 1999 at Snowbasin Ski Resort in Utah, when there was a hush in the patrol room. We were busy making bombs, checking avalanche transceivers, counting igniters and going over our avalanche control route plans. We were about to venture out onto the last three remaining control routes of the new ski area expansion to a peak called No Name. One complex route has a possible 37 bomb shots with several splits in the four-person team.

We were going out after a late start to Snowbasin's season. Two months of clear, cold weather had caused the half metre of snow on the ground to rot. Then a warm spell had caused a 2cm crust to form over the faceted sugar-like snow – it was one of the worst snowpacks Utah had ever seen. Then the snow came –150cm in a week. Tom, the snow safety officer, declared an extreme hazard. Natural avalanches were probable, human-triggered avalanches were certain. And both would be widespread and large enough to kill a group. A dangerous time to be going backcountry.

We ventured up the Porky Lift and waited for Frank to shoot some protection shots with an avalauncher mounted on the back of the snow groomer that we were standing on. The visibility was poor but it was good enough for us to see his bomb hit the ridge 3km away when the entire face cracked instantly, about 1km wide, in the blink of an eye. There was a massive avalanche 5-6m high and it was coming directly towards us. We positioned ourselves on a mound, and while two of our group leapt off the back of the snow groomer and ran for the trees, the rest of us watched in awe as the gigantic avalanche turned past us and smashed into the trees not far away.

Then it was our turn. We put on our skis and sidestepped into the fog to an avalanche path called the Swim Team Chute because of the numerous patrollers who had gone for a ride in an avalanche while controlling it. It required a strong arm to throw the bomb up the slope above the large tree you stood behind.

On one occasion the bomb landed on hard snow but didn't stick. It rolled back towards me and finished up sitting on my skis. I calmly picked up the burning bomb and tried again (they have a 90-second fuse), and I was thankful when it stuck in the snow high above us.

Once the bomb goes off you wrap your arms around the tree, with the second patroller holding onto your waist while the avalanche sweeps around the tree, well above your head. Truly exciting.

Opening day came around and we re-bombed all the areas to guarantee the public's safety. Half a metre of new snow came for opening day as well as big crowds – the skiing was awesome.

That was when I experienced one of the deepest powder runs of my life. I was skiing down a steep slope, snow bellowing over my shoulders, when it got even deeper and I disappeared completely under the surface of the snow. It was quite dark under the snow, and I had to jump every few turns to get my eyes above the snow surface and see if I was going to miss the upcoming trees. In 30 years of winters I've since skied very deep snow, flowing over my shoulders and face, but never this deep.

On a clear, calm day a week later we were getting ready to go to the No Name area. The senior patrollers were called in early. There was a strange quiet over the patrol room while we made our final preparations. It was an old portacom building; there were around 300 explosive charges on tables and in packs being quietly armed, everybody concentrating on their specific jobs. Each pack was labelled with who was to carry it. It was like a military operation.

Everyone knew their job and we got it done as briskly as possible.

It was still dark when the John Paul lift deposited us high up on the Wasatch Mountains. I loved being high in the mountains for sunrise. After a quick snow-mobile ride and a five-minute hike we were on top of No Name Peak. The view was breathtaking. We could see right down into Ogden and out to the Great Salt Lake. Brandt was tying the 15kg sack of ANFO onto the new bomb tram as the sun poked its head above the Uinta Mountains. The light was fantastic, causing a spectacular red haze in the sky. The sun was rising, there was soft white snow against the dark valley shadows. The mood was peaceful. I'm sure that this was one of those moments that cause many ski patrollers around the world to forget about the low pay rates and understand why they do what they do. At such times we all stop and just look for a minute in admiration.

The ANFO went off with an almighty boom, shaking the ground under us and knocking the snow from the trees. As we peered at the slope all we could see was a huge bomb crater with large circular cracks surrounding it. We'd had no result. We moved down to another new tram where we'd noticed large cones of snow built up on the uphill side of the trees. I ski cut onto the huge slope and poked my ski pole into the snow. When it hit ground less than 50cm down, we were sure that the slope had avalanched naturally. But we still had to be cautious as there might have been pockets which hadn't. Another team put another bag of ANFO on the Shooting Star slope and got the same result.

The rest of the control routes went well, and we achieved similar results. That day No Name was opened and after the weekend it was fully tracked out. It was no longer the backcountry experience it used to be. Nevertheless, I was glad I played a part in opening it.

Throwing bombs out of a helicopter is not something many people get to do during their lives. I used to love it, but nowadays I let others do it. I'm not sure why, maybe I asked myself too many times, 'What could possibly go wrong?'

In fact there are safety procedures, and in reality it is quite safe. The usual process is to put on a climbing harness and tie that to two solid points on the helicopter. The door is taken off and the helicopter is loaded with as many 10 to 20kg bombs as can be fitted in. Then you put double 90-second fuses on each bomb. The procedure is very military-like.

I once heard of a heli-bombing day in Canada years ago when a guy lit the bomb and threw it out the door. They waited for it to go off, which is normal procedure so you can check it has detonated, and also record the avalanche results. But after 60 seconds the pilot said that he could smell something burning, which is not that easy to do with the door off and wind circulating in the cabin.

The bomber looked down at the stack of bombs and realised he'd actually lit the bomb *below* the one that he'd thrown out. He quickly threw the lit one out and everything was fine. But that resulted in a procedure being developed in which the next bomb has to be moved to the door before it is lit. Or, even better, unlit bombs are put in a box with a lid.

Those types of near misses also led me in June 2002 to write the original standard operating procedures (SOP) for explosives use during avalanche control in New Zealand.

The weather isn't always good when you're heli-bombing. I remember a day when it was quite windy. I was tied in, standing on the skids, half out of the door, backside on the floor of the helicopter. We were hovering over the spot my colleague Anna in the front seat had chosen to place the bomb. I lit the bomb and checked for ignition by watching the fuse burn for a few seconds and then droop – an indication it was burning fine. But as I threw the bomb over the side, a violent gust of wind tipped the helicopter sideways and I didn't throw it properly. The 15kg sack of ANFO landed on the skid of the helicopter, just for a split second, long enough for me to suck in a breath and realise I'd have to untie myself then climb down and push the bomb off. Thankfully the bomb didn't straddle the skid for long; it rolled off and fell into the snow 50m below. We flew away and watched it go off.

It's a huge thrill watching a bomb release a powerful avalanche that races down the mountainside, billowing white clouds and scooping up more snow along the way, travelling at well over 100km/hr. Sometimes we'd chase it in the helicopter, flying just above it, tipped over slightly with the harness holding us in position, looking down into the depths of the avalanche. The power of nature is so evident, the beauty is mesmerising and watching it from a helicopter so close is an absolute buzz. When you forecast avalanches while guiding, the desired effect is you don't ever actually encounter one, and sometimes you question yourself for being too cautious. So to watch one from the safety of a helicopter, an un-survivable one that would rip your arms and legs from your torso without effort, is similar to an African park ranger giving a massive purring male lion a scratch under the chin.

There are many ways to deliver an explosive charge to a slope. There is a well-known saying that it takes 'the right bomb, in the right place, at the right time' to release an avalanche. The ideal spot to place the bomb is 1.2m above the surface of the snow at the point where the tension in the snowpack is the greatest. If an avalanche isn't released that is also a good sign as the vibrations shake the entire snowpack, compressing weak layers and consolidating unstable snow crystals.

Back at Snowbasin we were learning some new control routes after the owner had built several new lifts. It took 200 hand charges and 100 avalauncher shots to make the entire ski area safe to open. With fences and gates spread over the mountain, we'd open certain areas at a time, while still working on others.

Tom, the snow safety officer responsible for managing the avalanche programme, had an idea to speed things up while we were riding up the brand-new 15-person tram. He called the lift operators and asked them to stop it halfway to the top, right opposite the perfect bomb placement not far from the door. We unlocked the door, opened it, then confidently lobbed three bombs into the snow just a couple of metres away. Tom then called the lift operators and asked them to run the lift, taking us to the top and out of the way of the blast.

A few seconds went by and we were still not moving, but the 90-second fuses were burning. With raising panic and obvious stress in his voice, Tom called the lift operators again, explaining as politely as possible to please *run the fucking lift*.

They called back saying there was an electrical fault and it might take a few minutes. We stared at each other in alarm, then looked out of the door at the bomb fuses burning in the snow not far away. We were sitting in the brand-new tram car, not yet open to the public, thinking we were about to blow out the windows. We huddled on the floor with our backs to the bombs and stared at our watches as the timer counted down.

With a few seconds to go we covered our ears with our hands, as is standard practice, and braced for the explosion. Boom! The tram shook and was covered by exploding snow and black soot, but the windows stayed intact, as did our eardrums. A few seconds later the tram started moving and safely took us to the top. Tom decided that this system of delivering bombs to the slope should not be used again.

Sometimes we'd tape a hand charge to a single piece of bamboo for a stronger 'push' on the snowpack, more likely to cause an avalanche. One morning in an area called Sunshine Bowl, Tom had one ready to go. You wouldn't do this procedure until you'd thrown a few test shots. Sometimes you'd get no result from a bomb exploding, yet you knew there was an instability there which should avalanche. That meant an air blast could give you a better result, or at least you could be more confident that there wasn't an avalanche which could hit or smother a skier.

Tom skied carefully onto the slope we were concerned about, stuck the bamboo pole in the snow with the bomb taped to the top of it, 1.2 metres above the snow surface, pulled the igniter to light the bomb and did a kick-turn on his skis so he could return safely to the ridge where I was standing. A kick-turn is when you stand with your skis across the slope, then turn your downhill leg and ski 180°, step on it, then turn the other ski, thus turning on the spot.

I'd been telling him he should do the kick-turn before he lit the bomb, but he was the boss and with his typical humour told me to shove it. He probably regretted that because halfway through the kick-turn, with one ski pointing forward and one pointing backward, he fell forward, down the slope, with his legs split in opposite directions. He sank in the soft snow and was flailing around, trying to get to his feet so he could get back to the ridge.

The snow was deep, and he thrashed about, cursing loudly until he finally got to his feet and started moving towards the ridge. When he fell again, I knew the time was almost up on the fuse. I was safely on the ridge, not far away, so I leant over so he could grab my ski poles and I could try to pull him to safety. This was the position we were in when the bomb detonated, a few metres from our heads. Usually the snow will muffle the sound of an exploding bomb, but the air blast hit me like a punch in the head. As soon as it went off, we both froze, but thankfully the bomb didn't release an avalanche and Tom climbed back to the ridge. He wasn't the sort of guy who would have appreciated a smart comment at that point; I waited until later. We carried on down the rest of the control route in silence with my ears ringing loudly.

Ski cutting is another way to control avalanches and it was the reason for my second avalanche involvement (my first was on Mt Green on the Tasman Glacier). It's a fairly simple system: you jump on the snow, with enough forward momentum so that if the slope avalanches you can carry on skiing back to the safety of a ridge. We set off hundreds of avalanches that way. It was much quicker than throwing a bomb, but if you expected them to be big enough to hurt you, that's when you'd throw a bomb. You can also keep areas of the mountain open during a storm if you ski cut the small pockets as they build up during the day, thus preventing harmful avalanches developing.

To reach Middle Bowl Cirque required extreme skiing via a steep cliff band. I loved that stuff and always put up my hand to go and ski cut. Many ski patrollers were happy sitting around lift shacks during bad weather, but I loved being out in it, skiing the fresh snow and checking for pockets of snow that could develop into an avalanche.

I teamed up with another patroller called Hans and we skied carefully into the area one at a time. There wasn't too much new snow, so I skied down the steep slope in a big zigzag. The idea was to break up the slab formation by skiing it. I headed over to one side and sunk to my chest into a drift of snow. I knew instantly that I'd blown it. The snow released from the rocks above me and an avalanche started, taking me down with it, over a 3m cliff band, then another, and then into some large pine trees, which thankfully I missed. I felt stupid, though, being caught out like that.

But I'd hit my knee on a rock and it was really painful. I limped back to the base area and rested all the following day with a badly bruised knee. Lesson learnt! I was rostered on as dispatcher coordinating the patrollers from base over the radio, sending people to accidents, and generally logging what was going on where on the mountain. But most of the locals couldn't understand my Kiwi English.

18

MOUNT EVEREST

I was high in the Himalayas descending from the top camp after summiting a dramatic mountain called Ama Dablam (6812m) with an extremely heavy pack. I stayed near the back of our group, carefully watching the tired clients as they laboured under the weight of their own heavy packs, climbing awkwardly over the rocky terrain. I was ensuring they were doing okay and staying safe by clipping their safety leashes correctly to the fixed rope on the long technical descent.

We were at the top of the Yellow Tower, a feature of yellow rock and one of the two main technical difficulties on the climb. One of my clients was just about to clip in to a 30m vertical abseil down when I noticed that a Sherpa below was in trouble on the adjacent ascent rope.

He had swung out on the fixed rope, over the 1000m drop, then realised his pack was too heavy for him to climb the fixed rope with only one jumar (a device attached to the rope aiding vertical ascent). Most people use two jumars, so you can attach one to each foot and rest much easier. He was desperately holding onto the jumar, sweating and obviously freaking out. He couldn't move up or down.

He was looking up at me from 30m below, whispering, 'Help me, help me.' The Sherpa are incredibly proud and capable people in the mountains, so just seeing the desperation in his eyes and hearing it in his voice sent alarm bells ringing.

I asked my client to step aside, quickly clipped into the rope and abseiled down. My 25kg pack with a tent and my climbing gear made abseiling difficult and slow. I worked my way down to him just as his arms gave way and he flipped violently upside down, smashing forcefully into the rock wall and releasing a 'Yelp'.

The chest strap on his heavy pack slid up to his neck and was strangling him. I tried with all my strength, but I couldn't lift him back upright. The weight of my pack and his was just too much and as we were swinging in space my legs, which could only just touch the wall, were useless.

So I swung over to a crack and placed a piece of rock protection in it before hurriedly removing my pack and clipping it in. As I swung back, the Sherpa had started sliding out of his harness. When I got to him his harness was down at his knees. He was a second or two from falling out of it, 1000m to the glacier below.

I hauled him upright and helped him out of his pack. Together we lowered it back to his group, who were watching helplessly on a ledge below. Then he descended safely, albeit well shaken.

I didn't give doing this a second thought – you always help others in the mountains. I often wonder how I would have felt if he'd fallen while I was taking my pack off. Should I have just tossed it down the cliff immediately and not tried to hang it on the wall? I felt very proud that I had been able to help.

The only time in my life I'd felt like that before was when I was 11 or 12. My younger cousin had fallen out of a paddle boat in Australia and could not swim. We were a ways from shore and our parents were screaming. I calmly dove in, stopped him sinking and helped him back to his paddle boat. Saving someone's life is a very special feeling that is hard to explain.

I met the Sherpa a few days later in the valley. He was extremely grateful and tried to buy me beer after beer. I was just glad I had been in the right place at the right time. Like all Sherpas, he would have done the same for me. Thirty seconds later my client would have been abseiling the rope and I would not have been able to do anything except watch the Sherpa fall to his death.

My first expedition to the Himalayas had come in October 2003. It was an offer from a company called World Expeditions to guide a trip to two trekking peaks – Lobuche East (6119m) and Island Peak (6189m). I'd also paid US$500 to get my name listed on an Adventure Consultants Ama Dablam (6828m) climbing permit that was running at the same time.

Ama Dablam is the mountain on which I saved the Sherpa above. It's a dramatic, steep, technical mountain seen from most places in the Khumbu Valley with an imposing serac forming part of the top of the mountain. Ama Dablam means Mother's Necklace. The long ridges on each side are like the arms of a mother (ama) protecting her child, and the hanging glacier is thought of as the Dablam, the traditional double-pendant containing pictures of the gods that are worn by Sherpa women. Looking up at it from the valley creates a certain fear forming in your gut. It looks completely impossible to climb.

I was so excited to be going on my first trip to the Himalayas. I'd never been higher than 3724m, the height of Aoraki/Mt Cook and at that height in Nepal potatoes grow! I'd read about the mountains and the people, and I was ready to experience them. I took care to pack all the right gear, including camera and snack food, got my vaccinations and boarded a plane for Kathmandu.

The trekking peaks we were going to climb were pleasantly mellow and easy for beginner climbers. The other guide, Soren, had made several trips, but he wasn't a climber, nor did he have any guiding qualifications. He had a very autocratic manner about running the trip, which meant I had very little to do. I concentrated on enjoying the Himalayas and I even carried my 5kg SLR camera to the 6000m summit of Lobuche East, where I took many exceptional photos of Mt Everest and the surrounding peaks.

Two weeks into the expedition one member was struck down by high-altitude cerebral edema (HACE). He was unconscious and we had to put him in a Gamow bag. This is a hyperbaric chamber used to increase air pressure around the patient. The person is zipped inside, then the bag is pumped up. The pumping creates so much pressure inside that it is like going down 1000-2000m. He came right inside the chamber and we were able to put water, food, music and a pee bottle inside, but he had to be flown out.

That started my years of learning about the many different medical scenarios I'd have to deal with in remote situations. It was fun but also a challenge, which I enjoyed after my years of trauma training as a ski patroller. The next time I was to use a Gamow bag would be to save my mother's life some years later on the way to Mt Everest . . .

I also loved hanging out with the Sherpas; their modesty, humour, strength and loyalty were second to none. At camps after dinner I'd often leave the clients' tents to go and visit them. They'd be sitting tightly packed together in a small tent. 'Tashi delek' (a Tibetan greeting), I'd say from outside the zipped up tent and instantly the zip would be enthusiastically thrown open. Out would pop the friendly smiling worn face of a Sherpa, or two, waving me frantically inside. They always played cards and even though I couldn't understand what they were saying, or the game, we all laughed loudly at each other. They had an uncanny technique of throwing the card forcibly at the floor from as high as they could get in the tent, and it always landed the right way up in perfect position.

I'd arranged to leave the World Expeditions trip before the end so that I could attempt a solo climb of Ama Dablam. I left base camp on Island Peak at 1am and by sunrise I had climbed to the 6200m summit. It was an amazing feeling climbing alone high in the Himalayas, even if Island Peak was only a trekking peak. I was fit and had acclimatised well, moving fast alone in the dark over the lower rocky slopes. I dressed lightly so as to not sweat and carried only a very light pack.

I passed others quickly and got to the icy summit alone. It

was calm and cold, but I didn't feel lonely. I was exhilarated. The warm dawn sun rays bathed me, and even though I was on a 6000m summit, the almost 8000m summit of Mt Nuptse hung intimidatingly over me to the west. After a short rest I descended to base camp at a jog and later that evening was in a hot-solar shower in Dingboche at an altitude of 4410m. This is usually three days' walk from the summit.

The next day I headed down the valley loaded with a massive pack of gear and food for my Ama Dablam attempt. At Pangboche (4200m) I found a keen local porter to carry my pack up to Base Camp (4650m). I wanted to save my energy for the climb. It was always fun to hire locals and I enjoyed that interaction. The bartering over the price, the companionship on the climb, then the paying off (with a generous tip) at the end. He was happy to work, and I was happy to be without a pack and only NZ$10 poorer. We motored up to Base Camp with me having to half jog to keep up with him and my heavy pack.

I was hurrying because I wanted to try to reach the summit with a good friend Steve and his clients, for a bit of company and to see how the mountain was guided. But when I arrived at Base Camp I heard that they'd reached the summit that day. Oh well! I ate some of their good food and drank one of their beers and celebrated for them.

The next morning, I shouldered my heavy pack and headed off for Camp One, which was at 5400m. I was almost there when I passed Steve and his group coming down. I picked Steve's memory on details of the climb then carried on to the first camp. I was shattered by the time I reached the camp, but I forced myself to melt ice to make hot drinks and relaxed for the afternoon in the warmth of my tent. If I climbed the next day I would be able to meet them at Base Camp and accompany them down the valley.

Almost everyone who climbs Ama Dablam uses the three camps. To climb to the summit in one push from Camp One is tough, even if you're rested. I needed to go as light as possible so I left behind anything I didn't need. No camera, no bivvy bag, no stove. At midnight I was up and by 1am I was on the fixed ropes under a beautiful full moon. The climbing along the granite ridge was fantastic, even with the cold wind blowing across the ridge. The exposure was exciting as I swung out over an abyss while jumaring the vertical Yellow Towers. In the moonlight I could clearly make out the 1000m drop all the way to the valley floor.

Jumars are a mechanical device that you attach to the rope and are connected to your harness. There is a leg loop hanging from each one and you stand in one while sliding the other up the rope, then you stand in that one and slide the other up the rope. It is much easier if you're not carrying a heavy backpack, which pulls you backwards. If you need a rest, you can sit backwards and hang from your harness, which is also connected to the jumars. This is called jumaring. To give you the feeling of doing this at 5000m try stuffing two thick socks in your mouth and then run up some stairs!

About 4.30am I climbed onto the narrow ridge at 5750m where Camp Two was situated. This camp was like a bird's nest – a tiny area of semi-flat ground with several 100m drop-offs on all sides. The tents were tied in place with climbing rope and toileting was done by hanging one's backside over the edge. I tried not to step on any tent ropes, sneaking past the sleeping climbers tucked up in their warm bags. That was when I heard a tent zip open.

'Is that Mark?' shouted a familiar Kiwi voice. My friend Anna was awake early, and planning on climbing to catch the rest of her group at Camp Three for their summit push later that day.

'Want a cuppa tea?' she asked as I climbed into her tent. Sometimes, it's pretty cool when you bump into friends.

After a cup of tasty herbal tea, we decided to climb together. Anna had had a bad night's sleep, but she was starting to feel better. So as the sun sneaked over the horizon, we headed up to the steep ice-climbing above Camp Two on the Grey Towers.

As we climbed I had scenarios of Himalayan climbing bouncing around in my head – dodgy fixed ropes and altitude sickness. That made me anxious about trusting the thin Korean fixed lines on the steep 70-80-degree ice couloirs. But there was no option – you just had to be careful to pick the best-looking rope (there were sometimes several) and then trust it. 'Worry is a wasted emotion', I told myself and just relaxed climbing the ropes. The exposure was fantastic, and it was thrilling climbing while I chatted with Anna.

I'm sometimes asked whether relying on fixed ropes is safe. Fixed rope refers to a safety line that is attached to the mountain, their quality and strength varying significantly. In Nepal the Sherpas usually take the role of fixing ropes ahead of the climbers. They cut away old ropes and inspect the anchors. The ropes are supplied by the expeditions, and well-resourced expeditions usually provide good quality ropes, while cheaper operations provide rope a bit like an old shoelace. A guide's role is to evaluate these as best he or she can from below and if necessary either replace them or ask the Sherpas to.

There has to be a balance – a rope that is strong enough but not so heavy it can't be reasonably carried. Some ropes are just a hand line, with little weight on them, while others, like on Ama Dablam, are fully weighted and need to be of high quality. People have died from ropes breaking or from accidentally clipping into a rope that is not long enough or is not connected to the mountain at its other end. No one takes responsibility for them, and you have to decide yourself if you are prepared to take the risk of hanging from one.

As we went higher the wind grew stronger. Anna was cold – too cold – and snow was pluming off the summit. What to do? We got to the top of the ice-climbing, just below Camp Three at 6230m and found a flat rock in the sun and out of the wind. It was a few metres below the lee side of the ridge with ample room to sit comfortably, and we warmed up quickly.

'You feel better?' I asked her.

'Yes, but what about this wind?' she replied.

I agreed it was borderline and we decided to climb up to Camp Three and see how her group was doing; we'd see from there. It was pretty cool indeed, sitting there, high in the Himalayas, chatting in the warm morning sun.

After an hour or so we carried on. Camp Three wasn't far above and we climbed up the narrow snow arête towards it. When we got there, Anna's group were coming down, blown back from their summit attempt. They were on their way to Camp Two, to rest for another attempt when the weather improved.

I was sitting on the snow trying to keep still in the fierce wind that threatened to sweep me off the flat, wide snow slope which is Camp Three. I was sitting next to an abandoned tent that I didn't want to get into because it was only pegged down by small bamboo sticks. I thought it would soon be bound for the valley floor a few thousand metres downwind. What to do? Go up . . . or down?

My decision was, of course, up.

I set out alone across the snow towards the fixed ropes not far away. No sooner had I left the camp when a strong gust of wind pushed me flat onto the snow, pinning me there. My ice axe was dug into the firm snow to prevent my imminent death if I was blown off the slope.

I waited for the gusts to ease. You have to listen to nature in the mountains; you can fight for only so long, and I had done my best. For me, turning back from a summit is usually associated with relief. I've been pushing and pushing onwards. But I always keep a bit of paranoia front and centre in my mind when in the mountains. There are a lot of things trying to kill you. Still, I'm usually looking for reasons to go on, not a reason to turn back. But this time I was out of reasons to go up.

Down I went, all the way to Base Camp. A 2500m descent with a massive pack. Near the end of the trek my legs occasionally collapsed under me and I fell onto the dirt. I could have camped, but I was chasing my mate Steve down the valley and eventually I caught him in Tengboche, above Namche Bazar.

That night, celebrating with Steve and his team, I learnt an important Sherpa custom. If you've drunk enough and want to go to bed you leave your glass full. Not wanting to be rude, I kept trying to finish my glass of chang (potato wine), but Ang Tshering's wife Ang Tsemi refilled it as soon as I got anywhere near halfway through it. It was late when I stumbled out of the door, threw up in the garden outside and promptly passed out.

I wasn't too worried about missing the summit, because I

knew I'd be going back to guide for Adventure Consultants. I'd made sure I'd learnt enough in my solo attempt to strengthen my knowledge and improve my chances of being hired as a guide.

I went on to summit Ama Dablam three times. On the last occasion I was descending the summit in 2006 and waiting on a steep ice face, standing under the 'Dablam'. This is a big hanging ice-cliff near the summit. I was clipped into the fixed ropes waiting and watching my clients safely descend to me, when I felt an odd tingling sensation in my neck. It was as if all the hairs on my neck were sticking upright. It was weird, but I took note of it and moved away from under the ice-cliff. Nothing happened and we descended to Camp Three for the night.

Less than a week later, not far down the valley, we heard that a large piece of the Dablam had broken off and avalanched onto Camp Three, killing six climbers. Very sad indeed. That was my last time I climbed Ama Dablam.

I went on to guide several other expeditions to Nepal and Tibet – Island Peak (6189m), Lobuche East (6119m), Mera Peak (6476m), Cho Oyu (8188m) and finally Mt Everest. I loved working on big expeditions. Everything gave me a buzz – the guides, the Sherpas and other local staff, the logistics, the money transactions – and of course the summits.

In 2004 I led an expedition to Mera Peak for World Expeditions with a group of 12 clients. As many groups are, they were an odd bunch, but some lifelong friendships came out of it. It was a month-long trek to climb the highest trekking peak in Nepal at 6500m. The group mostly got on well, but on day 15 one of the members, a pretty young woman in her mid-20s, came to me that night to have a word. She had a problem. One member of the group had the hots for her. He was a boring, mildly overweight, bearded tax collector in his mid-to-late 40s. This was never going to go well.

Apparently earlier that day when she stopped and ducked off the trail for a toilet stop, he had hung back. When she finished she had found him standing facing her with his pants around his ankles and his hands on his hips, while he waved his penis at her.

She hid her face with her hand and walked past him briskly to catch up with the rest of the group. I was horrified.

I pulled the guy aside and explained that that sort of behaviour was completely unacceptable on an expedition and that I'd kick him off if it happened again. He apologised half-heartedly and said he thought she liked him. I suggested a different approach next time he thought a girl liked him! The ironic thing was that as most of us had already found out by getting to know her, she had a partner – and she was gay.

The Mera Peak expedition travelled to an isolated valley and in those years the Maoists were fighting the Nepal Government. We'd heard about this and my trip brief had warned me about it too. There were Maoist flags hanging in many towns and sometimes I could tell that our staff were nervous in these towns. We saw a few rough-looking guys who were obviously Maoists walking around carrying rudimentary weapons. One such weapon was a baseball bat-like stick with large nails protruding from the end. On another occasion we were hiking along the trail and we found a homemade revolver which had massive 303 bullets in the chamber. Those bullets were more suited to a rifle, not a handgun. We took it to the next town and left it with the locals, who were very thankful.

I remember well the day I was about to have tea in a remote mountain teahouse near a high pass when a small, well-dressed man sat down next to me and gave me a cup of tea. He introduced himself politely and said he was from the Maoist Party and would I like to make a donation? I was about to laugh when I realised I was being politely robbed. If I'd said no, his cohorts, who were most likely hiding in the bushes nearby, would probably have beaten up our local staff.

I asked him how much I should 'donate' and he suggested a moderate amount. I assumed it was a negotiation, the same as when you buy something in a shop, so I suggested a smaller amount. He said that wouldn't be suitable and suggested a figure between the two. I agreed. I paid the ransom, about NZ$10 per person, and drank my tea. He was just about to leave when I asked if it was possible to have a receipt.

'Of course,' he said and smiled proudly as he pulled out his receipt book. It took 10 minutes for him to neatly write out the receipt and stamp it with an official-looking stamp. All this went on while my clients nearby were drinking their own tea. When I told them later we'd been robbed, they were shocked. They'd thought I was just chatting to a random local.

A few days later when it happened again and I was approached by another Maoist, I produced my receipt and said I had already given a donation. He studied it then smiled, thanked me for our support and wished me a good day.

I was held up by the Maoists a few more times during my Himalayan career, but it was always a fun and non-threatening occasion. I'd negotiate, get a receipt and be polite to them. We never had any trouble and it usually gave the clients a good story to take home.

When I arrived in Lukla the military had somehow found out about my run in and had come to get me in the teahouse. They took me into the dungeon of a jail where a poor guy was locked up in the dark, wet confines. They asked me if he was the guy who had robbed me. He wasn't, but even if he had been I'm not sure I would have said so. It seemed pretty obvious they were looking for an excuse to shoot him.

The Maoists became more and more brazen over the years and eventually had 'donation' checkpoints even in the busy Khumbu Valley. Later they eventually formed a legitimate political party and won seats in parliament.

I'd heard stories, read books and seen the movies on Tibet. I knew it wouldn't be as nice as Nepal. While various cultures flourish in Nepal, the Chinese have smothered alternative cultures in Tibet. I also knew it was more arid than Nepal; being on the lee side of the Himalayas, it received much less rain.

My first trip to Tibet was also my first expedition to an 8000m mountain called Mt Cho Oyu. I was working with Mike – I did many trips with him and learnt a lot. He was an amazing mentor.

We flew from Kathmandu to Lhasa, then spent a few days in Land Rovers driving over the partially constructed highway to Mt Everest until we came to what is known as Chinese Base Camp (5100m), where we spent some time acclimatising and running our clients through fixed-rope training.

We filled our packs for a two-hour walk above camp to a rock face Mike had used before. When he became distracted while loading his pack and walked off, I thought it would be funny to put a large rock weighing two to three kilos in the base of his pack. He came back, threw his pack on his back and charged up the hill without even noticing the extra weight. Horrified, I followed the rest of our group, and forgot about the rock as we spent the day training before we descended to our camp.

We were unpacking outside the tent when I heard the roar of anger as Mike lifted the rock from the base of his pack. His face was red and his dark eyes were flashing. Mike is well over 2m tall, so when he stood up and charged towards me with the rock in his big hands, I took off around the tent at a sprint with him in hot pursuit. We had gone only about 30 to 40m when the altitude hit us and we stopped, bent over and puffing. Thankfully, he laughed about the rock. For a split second I thought I'd gone too far, but Mike is a gentle giant and forgot about it quickly. Although from time to time I checked inside my pack for rocks during the rest of the trip, never quite relaxing until we were back in Nepal at the end of the expedition.

The trip went astonishingly well and we summited using oxygen on 26 September. The view of Mt Everest from the top of Cho Oyu is one of the best, with a unique angle looking right into the guts of the Western Cwm (on the standard climbing route). The arid, dry planes of Tibet to the west were a stark contrast from the snow-capped mountains of Nepal to the east. I still had constant dreams about climbing Mt Everest and hoped this would come to fruition.

Finally, Guy had offered me a job on Mt Everest. In March 2007

I arrived in Kathmandu two weeks before the clients with Guy and Luis (Luis was an American guide I did several trips with). There were all sorts of jobs to be done – clear the equipment sent from New Zealand through customs, buy truckloads of food and fuel, sort and pack it all into porter loads (20kg) and test and fix all the expedition electrical equipment.

On my first trip to Aconcagua in 2003-04, I made sure I learnt how to send the dispatches. This required computer skills and patience. I had to create an interesting story, spellcheck (not my strong point), find a photo from the day, resize it, connect the satellite phone, find a signal, then quickly send it before either the signal was lost or the batteries went flat. All that had to be done after a day of guiding while I was lying in a tent feeling exhausted. In the end I became good at it and I'm sure it helped my inclusion on expeditions over the years. Some guides hated it and couldn't have done it to save their lives. Often they welcomed my help.

During all my expeditions to Nepal (about 12) I succumbed to bad food poisoning only twice. When I say bad, I mean so bad you are not sure if you should be sitting on the toilet or kneeling in front of it with your arms wrapped around the base and your head in the bowl. You never want to move more than a few metres away and it's usually hell for 24 hours.

On one such occasion I had to go to the Ministry of Tourism to pay our expedition fee, which was usually several thousand dollars. I remember gingerly walking into the meeting and being thankful the couch had a clear-plastic cover over it. I had to drink milky tea from a dirty cup and make small talk with the minister while he issued our permit. To them it is a formal process that couldn't be rushed; for me, sweating and shaking and on the verge of crapping my pants, I just wanted either to die or go back to my hotel room. It was a few days later until I could fart with confidence again . . .

The trek to Everest Base Camp takes about 12 days. I was leading a group of trekkers that included my mum and my uncle. Jo was there also, trekking with two friends. She doesn't do well on Nepali food and the night before she left had the trots. I was distracted by my group, so I never really had time to be sympathetic and sent her on her way a day ahead of our group.

A guide always gives a brief at the start of the trip. I say things such as, 'Tell me if you are taking any medication, make sure you wash your hands often, sneeze into your elbow (not your hand), drink a lot of fluids,' and so on. The trick on an expedition is to keep everyone healthy.

It was day seven or eight when I noticed Mum wasn't acclimatising well. In fact really poorly. I was worried about her as she was showing signs of high-altitude cerebral edema. When I walked into her dark room in the teahouse with its small window in the paper-thin walls, there was vomit on the floor between her bed and her friend's. Mum was unconscious on her bunk. With a little panic in my voice I shook her gently by the shoulder and she woke, but was slurring her words, only opening her eyes when I spoke to her. And she had a very low oxygen saturation (you can measure it with a small device called a pulse oximeter). Normal pulse oximeter readings usually range from 95 to 100%. Values under 90% are considered low. On high altitude expeditions you can drop into the 70s. Mum's oxygen saturation was in the mid-50s! I had to act fast.

I put her in the Gamow bag. Once she was inside and we'd lowered the altitude by increasing the air pressure around her, she became alert again and I was able to question her and figure out why she was not acclimatising. Our programme was designed with the right time to adjust, so clients would not get sick. I asked her if she was sure she wasn't on any medication.

'No, none at all, just my sleeping pills,' she replied. I worked it out instantly. Most sleeping pills suppress your breathing, which at sea level is no problem. But at high altitudes this often causes issues. I scolded her for not telling me, and she told me off for not mentioning that sleeping pills were medication, but we got over it. I gave her some Diamox, and she quickly came right and managed to carry on to Everest Base Camp a few days later. At one point, I thought I'd be booking her for a medical evacuation via helicopter.

Once we arrived at Base Camp (5400m) it was Jo's turn. She'd contracted acute mountain sickness (AMS). She stayed there for a few nights and came right while Mum and the other trekkers headed back to Kathmandu.

We had our puja ceremony, which is performed to contact the divine Sagarmatha and pray for a safe expedition. Then at 2am our head Sherpa, Ang Tshering, burnt juniper and we walked around the makeshift stone altar clockwise tossing rice over our left shoulders to pay our respects to the Buddhist gods. We then left for the Khumbu Icefall for our first acclimatisation trip.

Jo would be leaving that morning while we were climbing and I bawled my eyes out. The emotion of Jo leaving, the long expedition ahead and the joy of starting the climb overwhelmed me. Although she was excited to be going down to thicker air and warmer temperatures, she was also in tears as we hugged goodbye for the next six to seven weeks. We didn't talk much, just a smile and a small wave.

The Khumbu Icefall was for me the hardest part of climbing Everest. I found crossing the ladders over deep crevasses absolutely terrifying. I was lucky because my feet are big, which meant my toes were on one rung while my heel was on the other. People with small feet had to balance the arch of their foot on one rung of the ladder, which was far less stable. However, many of the crevasses were much wider than one 5m ladder, so two or sometimes three ladders would be tied together with what looked like old bale twine, or very weak-looking rope. The ice also melted where the ladders touched at each end, so that one side would be lower than the other, tipping the ladder sideways. There were rope handrails to clip onto for safety and also to hold onto for balance. But these were tied at ground level, so you had to lean forward to keep tension on them without any additional balance help. It didn't help either that the crevasses were deep. Very deep. Often the bottom was not visible, just cold darkness.

If you climb in New Zealand you do everything in your power to stay well away from icefalls like the Khumbu, because they are so dangerous. But glaciation at lower altitudes and in warmer climates moves much faster.

On our first trip up the icefall we encountered several obstacles.

I named one such obstacle 'the valley of doom', because it required climbing down a ladder into a crevasse, then crossing a wobbly three-ladder bridge over a crevasse so deep all you could see was black below. Towering above the ladders was a huge leaning ice tower which looked as if it could collapse at any second, crushing and sending whoever was on it to the depths of the crevasse.

To top that off, at around 6000m you *cannot* walk fast, so moving underneath this tower seemed to take forever. You had to keep your fear and frustration in check. Clients would move slowly, people in front would too. You didn't have the pace to pass people. If you rushed it would result in losing your breath and the frustration would boil up. I'd say to myself, 'Breathe,' and take long slow breaths to keep calm and just accept the risk was there.

I'd often go ahead a bit and wait in a safer spot for the clients to catch up. The critical points to do with crevasses were safety, and you'd often pick up a client's carabiner not done up right, or a harness too loose.

Tragically, on 18 April 2014 a serac collapsed, resulting in an ice avalanche into the Khumbu Icefall that killed 16 climbing Sherpas.

You breathe easier mentally, not physically, once you climb out of the icefall into the Western Cwm and reach Camp One. We rested for the afternoon, then the next day we walked a little further before another night and the descent to Base Camp for a rest. There is a lot of rest involved when you climb Mt Everest. You have to let your body adjust. I think we climbed for about 10 to 12 days on a typical six-week Everest expedition. Cards were one of the best pastimes and entire days might go by while I played games of 500.

On the next trip we went to Camp Two at 6500m where we had a very comfortable dining tent with chairs, tables and a chef. The Camp Two cooks put out tablecloths, fake flowers, snacks and hot thermoses of tea. There was an LPG heater and the tent skin was thick, keeping the temperature inside nice and warm. We had LPG lights and speakers for music, and the cooks would prepare things like bacon, scrambled eggs and muffins (with bacon brought from New Zealand), pancakes, toasted sandwiches, nachos, spaghetti bolognaise, chicken and pasta, pizzas and even sushi.

But climbing at high altitude is like having a hangover. You always feel a little off-colour and your appetite is suppressed. I was always quite lucky because I didn't get headaches. I've never suffered from headaches, not even at home. I don't lose my appetite and I can sleep like the dead. These are the three things which affect most people, especially Guy, who would sometimes throw up at high altitude.

From Camp Two we climbed the Lhotse Face, a steep slope of hard blue ice and fixed ropes. Camp Three is halfway up this face and the tents are erected on small platforms painstakingly cut from the ice. One side is hacked into the face and the resulting bits of ice are stacked to form the outside support for that half of the tent. You have to be very careful walking around and it's just as well there are fixed-rope handrails for things like going to the toilet. I've heard a story of a Sherpa at Camp Three who left his tent with only his inner boots on, slipped down the icy Lhotse face and died.

After sleeping at Camp Three we descended all the way to Pheriche, a village a long day's walk down the valley. Being down near 4000m allowed appetites to return and rest to come easy. It was warm and comfortable, so we rested for a week, watching the long-range weather forecast and waiting for our summit window. We read books, played cards and ate. Eating was our most popular pastime – we ate four meals a day trying to rebuild our strength for the summit push. Well-funded expeditions like ours spent thousands of dollars on weather forecasts, whereas the budget companies just watched us and followed us up. We watched the weather and waited.

People often ask me about the crowding you see in photos of Everest climbers. I get a bit cynical as they usually live in cities with long queues of rush-hour traffic. Many of those busy days are caused by budget companies not having enough oxygen and food to enable them to spread out their summit attempts. Meetings take place between all expedition leaders who outline their summit plans in an attempt to try and spread everyone out on the mountain. But then some groups change their plans and go when it's busy and cause the queues to build up.

Another problem arises because it doesn't take much to slow down a queue. Sadly many clients aren't capable enough mountaineers to unclip from the ropes and pass someone who is moving too slowly. Guides don't want them doing that. Some people are also extremely arrogant and don't step aside to allow others to pass. Passing someone takes some time too when you think about the speeds we go at. It's a bit like an old tortoise passing another older tortoise.

So go easy on the climbers who choose to climb Mt Everest. I detest it when people criticise what others do. Sure, Everest has been done before, but in the early days when Hillary and Tensing climbed it, almost 100 people helped to put two people on the summit. These days expeditions try and put everyone on the top.

After our rest we headed to Base Camp and rested for a couple more days, then climbed to Camp One, then Camp Two, rested a day, then up to Camp Three, where we slept on oxygen. That helped with appetites, warmth and sleep. Then we climbed to the final camp, Camp Four on the South Col. This is where you start to feel as if you are in space. Everything is an effort – getting out of the tent, going to the toilet, eating. We rested for the afternoon and tried to sleep, mostly unsuccessfully.

At 10pm we got up and started getting ready. We wanted to leave camp at 11pm. Chuldum, our Camp Four cook with a cigarette hanging from his lips, delivered thermoses of boiling water before that. 'Sherpa oxygen,' he'd reply when I laughed at him. Did you know that water boils at a third of the temperature at 8000m that it does at sea level? I tentatively dipped my fingers into the boiling water and was pleasantly surprised when it didn't burn. We filled our water bottles with hot water, drank tea, and tried to stomach oats, or anything we could eat. Above 8000m your body cannot replace muscle tissue; it eats it up instead. Our bodies were pretty much dying and there was nothing we could do except get on with the climb.

We started climbing slowly, very slowly, in the dark, lonely hours of the long night. Everyone had an oxygen mask on, so conversation was limited. Guy, Luis and I were the guides, with eight clients as we'd had to turn one back. He'd climbed all day without eating, then collapsed in the final hours of the day. We couldn't trust him to get to the summit and back again safely. To each client at the summit briefing we'd say, 'On summit day we are working for your family, not you!' Also with us were 12 climbing Sherpas, one for each person, plus a spare.

Another two or three groups spotted us leaving and rushed to follow us up the mountain. A few hours into climbing the Triangular Face we were all clipped into a piece of shitty-looking rope – there must have been 30 to 40 people on one section (I was doing the calculations in my head). The rope's breaking strength must have been about 600kg. If each person was putting 15-20kg of weight on the rope, that was near breaking strain. I changed my body position, stopped pulling on the rope and walked upright.

It happened soon after that. The rope above us snapped and the weight of all the people below impacted on us. We knew the rope had broken and resisted the pull from below by holding onto the rope, but there were 20 or so climbers below who had no idea the rope had broken and were still leaning heavily on it, resting and waiting for the people in front to move. Yelling with an oxygen mask on doesn't resonate very far and it took a few terrifying moments for the message to get back. Plus some quick thinking by Guy as he ripped off his gloves, quickly re-tied the rope ends together and put his gloves back on before his hands got frostbite.

We carried on climbing and for the next few hours we had one of the most magical views of a storm I have ever witnessed. The valley 3000m below was filled with dark puffy clouds and Base Camp was under these clouds. Within the clouds was an electrical storm. White bolts of lightning were lighting up the underside of the clouds. It was like watching a storm from the position of a god in heaven. It was totally mesmerising.

By dawn we were at the top of the Triangular Face and it was time to change our oxygen bottles. Next was the South Ridge towards the South Summit. As the sun came up another sight took my attention – the grey shadow of Mt Everest, a massive, dark, triangular shape, reflected onto the bulbous white clouds below. After watching this amazing shadow for a few minutes, it dawned on me that I was near the top of that shadow. I was starting to get excited, we were actually climbing Mt Everest! We were doing it.

Onwards and upwards, one step, three to four breaths then another step. Moisture from my oxygen mask was dripping onto my SLR camera (with a 35mm slide film in it) and freezing on the top, rendering the control adjustments useless. I had to shoot photos on automatic – the red sunrise over Makalu, the shadow of Mt Everest, the clients climbing up behind me in the clear, crisp glow of a mountain sunrise, the bright white snow, the colourful down suits of the climbers, the sun so bright you couldn't look directly at it for long, the deep blue 8000m sky. I was loving it. Taking it all in.

I was also remembering to watch the clients carefully, checking for signs of altitude sickness. I had a syringe of dexamethasone pre-loaded in my breast pocket. I also had to check they were clipping into the ropes correctly and had their crampons securely on their feet. I had to make sure no skin was showing, because frostbite would take only a minute or two. I couldn't forget reminding them to snack and drink water. We'd filled our water bottles with boiling water before leaving camp, and with the bottles tucked inside a neoprene sleeve, they had stayed warm. On top of all that there was watching the weather and talking to Guy and Luis over the radio. They were at the front, while as a junior guide I was near the back.

I never really thought too much about whether I'd reach the summit or not. Of course I wanted to, but as a guide you don't get your hopes too high. Your first priority is the safety of the clients; if one had had a medical condition, I could well have ended up taking him or her down.

We reached the South Summit at about 7am. The day was ideal.

We took a rest to check on everyone, change oxygen bottles and check the levels. We needed enough oxygen to get to the summit and back, including any unforeseen delays. It was then that much to my surprise one client, Chuck, decided to turn back. He was quite experienced and strong, but he never rested during acclimatising days. So like many similar clients on Mt Everest he had tired too soon, although he could have probably pushed on and made it. I liked Chuck and would have tried to talk him into continuing, but Luis chatted to him and announced that he was turning back.

I was getting ready to leave, falling into my position at the back of the group, when Guy turned to me and asked if I wanted to lead the group from then on.

'Hell yeah,' I said and headed along the exposed traverse towards the Hillary Step, a feature I'd heard about all my life. It didn't look too high or difficult. That is by today's standards – it was a completely different story when Ed climbed it back in 1953. Technical climbing standards were far lower then and because no one had ever done it, it carried that mystique of 'Can it be done?'

At the foot of the Step, I clipped my safety carabiner into the rope and my jumar. Even so, I wanted to climb the Hillary Step under my own steam and see how hard it was. So I never pulled on my jumar, just slid it up the rope level with me in case I fell. I moved one foot up after the other, ensuring I placed the spikes of my crampons on small edges in the rock, with my other foot cramponing into the firm snow to the right. This was bridging as Hillary described in his book. 4-5m up I looked down between my legs at the fall I'd take if I slipped, but I felt secure, my axe was in the firm snow, my jumar was on the rope and my left hand was on the rock.

I made a few more moves while I watched the client behind me clip into the fixed rope, attach his jumar and start up the rope. I pulled myself over onto the top of the Step, clipped in my carabiner for safety and leant over to watch the clients climb up behind me. I was quietly stoked I'd climbed the Hillary Step under my own steam and watched as the clients struggled to climb behind me.

I took out my camera (I had it stored in a bum-bag in front of me) and snapped some of the most amazing photos of my life, looking back at the South Summit and down at climbers coming up the Step.

As soon as a couple of the clients were close behind me, I turned towards the summit and slowly plodded on. Emotions started welling up inside me. One minute I was crying my eyes out, the next I was laughing loudly under my oxygen mask. It finally dawned on me that I was going to summit Mt Everest.

I knew the top was close. I could hear the cooks and Base Camp staff talking on the radio. They knew we were close. They were banging pots and pans loudly over the radio. I knew Jo was back home on the phone to Base Camp and that she too knew how close I was.

Crying, laughing, crying, laughing, checking the clients, step, breath, step, swing around and take a photo, breath, step and then the final steps . . .

I was there! 8850m on the summit of Mt Everest. High fives with my Sherpa friends, hugs with Guy, Luis and the clients. Tears. Laughter.

When I wandered over to look down the Tibet side into China, I spotted a friend from Queenstown standing there. Woody had just summited too. We said hi and chatted about normal stuff like home and salads, the food you crave most while you're on a big mountain.

Our clients couldn't believe that we could just bump into a Kiwi friend on the summit of Mt Everest. The funny thing was the next time I bumped into Woody we were on a commercial flight at about the same elevation!

We monitored the clients, checked the oxygen and enjoyed ourselves for about 40 minutes. As everyone knows, the summit is only halfway. I went to change the film in my SLR and after opening the new roll I simply tossed it over the side of the mountain down into Tibet. As soon as I'd done it, I realised how stupid it was and promptly put my oxygen mask back on and took some deep breaths. During those few minutes without oxygen, taking photos and chatting on the summit, my level of consciousness must have dipped. Luckily I recognised it, put a new roll of film in my camera and wound it on. It was time to leave.

Guy was looking after one of our clients who wasn't getting enough oxygen. To alleviate the problem, they swapped masks and regulators. The client also had a retinal bleed and couldn't see clearly. Guy and two Sherpas helped him down. Fortunately, his condition improved relatively quickly as he descended.

Tired but extremely happy, I escorted the stronger clients at the front of the group back to Camp Four at the South Col. I was quietly happy to be going down first, I must admit I was a little strung out being so high above 8000m and having to look after people. The safety margins are thin. I knew it was only the oxygen and time that was keeping me alive. Guy and Luis were far more experienced than me and it showed. They took their time at the back with the weaker clients. It was a warm, sunny day and I hadn't worn my down pants all day, although I must run hot as I was the only one not wearing them. We got back to camp about 3pm, drank soup and tea and relaxed for the afternoon.

The mountain had been busy that day, but we were the first group and had left early to avoid bottlenecks. There is only one Everest; sure it can be busy, but for most people problems are often self-inflicted and caused by choosing a budget trip, with no backup and not enough oxygen or support.

We ended up providing resources – Sherpa and food – to help carry down a Nepal expedition team member who had been abandoned by her group on summit day when she collapsed from altitude sickness. Her team either didn't care or weren't prepared to turn back and help. We also found people sleeping in our tents because their agent had promised tents that weren't there. Guy was happy to give them some feedback and point out it was check-out time!

The world is getting busy, it is overpopulated and, yes, Everest can be hectic. The biggest mountain in almost every country is overcrowded; if you want a remote climbing experience it is incredibly easy to find a distant mountain with no one on it. You can even find a mountain that has never been climbed.

But there is only one Everest, and each person still has to climb it one step at a time. They go through hardships and suffering. They vomit, have headaches and loss of appetite, sleeplessness, no showers for a week or more, severe cold, desert-like heat, cramping legs, aching shoulders, avalanches, crevasses, altitude risks and time away from families – to name a few.

But the rewards of climbing Mt Everest are lifelong. The pride and confidence you take into life from then on, the satisfaction of knowing you did it and, as a guide, the professional recognition you carry onwards in your career are always there. I have been asked over a hundred times in my life if I've climbed Everest, and I know they were expecting me to say no. I always enjoy the unexpected astonishment on their faces when I quietly reply *yes*. Especially when it comes from a slightly arrogant person who thinks of themself as a climber.

They ask, 'Have you been to the Himalaya?' and I usually just say, 'Yes, a few times.' Then they might ask, 'To Everest?' and I say, 'Yes.' Then they often say they've also been to Everest Base Camp. I stay quiet, and eventually they ask more until they figure out I was actually climbing the mountain and got to the top. It was not the hardest climb I ever completed, but it is the easiest mountain to tell people about and become immediately respected as a mountaineer.

Back at Base Camp we had a fantastic party. But I'd lost 10kg on the expedition and my body couldn't handle the amount of alcohol I drank. I ended up vomiting out the end of my tent, thus completing the grand slam of vomiting at all five camps on the mountain.

The next day I walked down to Pheriche with clients who wanted to fly back to Kathmandu in a Russian MI6 helicopter. There was a free seat for me, so that afternoon I was tucked up in my favourite restaurant in Kathmandu with a glass of red wine and a Caesar salad.

I'd taken a damaged oxygen bottle back with me and removed the top so that you could see into the bottle. Inside Kathmandu Airport the eyes on the security guy scanning the bags almost popped out of his head when he saw the bottle on the x-ray. He opened my bag and looked into the end of the bottle where I had a US$20 note stashed. He took the note, looked inside the bottle and closed the bag with a smile and a wink.

I moved on to check-in, where I think it was the only airport left in the world where they still had handwritten baggage tags. After weighing my heavy bags, the airline attendant explained, with a sympathetic expression, that I had too much luggage and it would cost US$450. I was prepared for that scenario too and had a US$50 note rolled inside the palm of my hand. I rested my hand on his side of the counter with the note just protruding from my fingers and asked if that would help. He looked left, then right, then reached out and took it from my hand and slipped it into his breast pocket.

'Of course, and I'll also give you an upgrade,' he said.

19

STARVED AND TRAPPED

It was spring in Wanaka. I was working in the Adventure Consultants office when an exciting opportunity came up to go to Carstensz Pyramid, on the western central highland's end of the Papua Province in far eastern Indonesia. Carstensz Pyramid is one of the Seven Summits, the highest mountain on each of the seven continents. A large part of my work over the years has been involved with guiding and organising expeditions to these mountains. It's worth noting that the western part of Papua is not part of the country known as Papua New Guinea (PNG), which most New Zealanders know of. It is in fact part of Indonesia.

Western Papua has been plagued by political unrest over the years. Of course we considered this when planning the expedition and hired the best local operator we could find. Not an easy task when the operator Guy had used the year before was now in jail. It was hard to tell who to trust. We got all the permits from the Indonesian Government with the assistance of our agent, and I boarded a flight with my climbing gear, expedition food and a pocket full of US dollars for unplanned expenses and maybe some bribes to help grease the expedition wheels. I also packed my kitesurfing gear for a few days' rest afterwards in Bali, where the expedition was to end.

I met my client, Jamie, from Canada, in Jakarta just before the end of 2007. He was a tall, fit-looking guy who was a professional motivational speaker. He had a good sense of humour and a great laugh, so we got along well straightaway.

After taking off from Jakarta we flew most of the night towards Papua, island hopping. Each landing was initially dark and deserted and sometimes we'd get off to wait at an empty departure gate, while at other times we'd sit on the plane. A few people would get off and a few would get on. No one seemed in a hurry. Once the sun rose, we had views of small islands and a tropical blue ocean speckled with small fishing boats.

Jets didn't fly to the small runway on Papua, so we changed to a turbo-prop plane for our last jump to get there. While the majority of Indonesians are Asian in origin and appearance, the Papuans are almost African in appearance. Their friendliness and genuine intrigue was immediately apparent as our agent Ben met us at the airport and drove us to the only hotel in the town of Nabire in the remote north-west of the province. The hotel was extremely basic with just a few rooms, each with a creaky ceiling fan, cold shower, hard bed and dirty tile floor with cockroaches and spiders everywhere. The heat was stifling and the humidity as close to 100% as was environmentally possible, until later in the day when the sky darkened and torrential rain poured down for an hour.

Initially the locals looked angry and intimidating to us. I'm not sure why, but their very black skin mixed with rough clothes, toned muscular bodies, unshaven faces and dark eyes created a look that I wasn't used to. I assume now that it was an unfair stereotype that western culture had engrained into us. When I waved and smiled, they broke into broad grins and frantically waved back, giggling to their friends. I later realised that the only white people they'd ever seen were in movies and in magazines, so we would have looked like movie stars. And maybe we looked intimidating to them as well.

We walked around the slum-like town with its dirt roads, carless streets, small tin roof houses with barely any walls that housed small families, and roadside shops covered with tarpaulins. It was busy with some people going about their business and others hanging out in groups on the streets chatting and laughing. They seemed happy although they had very little in the way of material possessions. The wealthy ones had motorbikes and there was often an entire family of five travelling on one small motorbike.

We were there to climb Carstensz Pyramid, or Puncak Jaya as the locals refer to it. It is 4884m high and probably remains the most remote and least visited peak on the Seven Summits journey. This is because it has exceedingly difficult access. On one side is the Freeport Mine, one of the largest gold and copper mines in the world. An American company employs around 20,000 people to work in this massive operation and does not under any circumstances allow tourists to pass through it to reach the mountain. On the other three sides there are kilometre upon kilometre of untouched jungle inhabited by tribes of Papuans who have rarely been visited by the western world and who still occasionally practise cannibalism. I was told they don't often eat Europeans; they prefer to eat their enemies after a battle.

We spent one night in Nabire, where our agent had to complete our logistics as well as those for four independent climbers. We got together on New Year's Eve for dinner in a small restaurant in the busier part of town. It was full of locals (my usual technique for eating in foreign places is to pick somewhere the locals are eating), and they all stopped talking and stared as we entered the small establishment. The entry was past a homemade 44-gallon drum-style barbecue on the side of the dirt street. The restaurant had mud-brick walls with large glassless windows. It was furnished with small square tables and school-style chairs which sat on the bare concrete floor. It looked as if it had been recently hosed out and was relatively clean. The lighting was an old, weak, basic light bulb in the middle of the room, which was casting long, dark shadows. When I looked around the room dozens of dark black faces stared back at me with bright white teeth showing near perfect smiles.

The restaurant had no menu, but it seemed to serve tasty-looking fresh fish and some un-appetising-looking options such as a well-barbecued foot of sheep or dog, something that looked like roast cockroaches and what we guessed was cow's brain. We pointed to the fish and we were served a bony, but fresh small fish with rice and a smile from the waiter. I never really know how healthy or hygienic a meal is until the night has passed and I go to the toilet in the morning. In India I always joked about how you should pop the toilet paper in the fridge before you go to bed in case you get the 'double burn'! But the next morning everything was fine. A short time later we met another group of people that the agent was also helping get to the mountain.

We were an unlikely bunch. There was a Canadian woman, an Irishman and two Englishmen. The British threesome were not your typical mountain climbers. They were cigar-smoking, beer-drinking, out-of-shape pub dwellers. We watched them with intrigue as they bumbled with their climbing gear and hunted unashamedly for beer in the Muslim town.

'That is shocking,' Jamie said to me. 'Why are they here?' The Indonesian Government has banned alcohol in Papua due to its disastrous effects on the local population from loss of consciousness and engaging in acts of domestic violence and crime. The locals couldn't cope with alcohol, so the island was alcohol free – unless you were from the UK, it seemed.

Our plan was to charter a Bell 212 helicopter and fly into Base Camp at 4200m. It was malaria and dengue country, so we were taking medication and covering up to avoid mosquito bites. The British didn't seem aware of that and wandered around in shorts and tee shirts and were therefore bitten all over. Over dinner we found out that the helicopter needed a small repair and we wouldn't be flying the next day as planned. As we had nothing else to do, we went to the beach for a swim. It was a sweltering 35°C with 100% humidity, so a swim sounded a great way to pass the time.

Three days, three swims and three excuses later we were still in Nabire. It felt as if we'd never get to the mountain. When we finally found out that the machine was fixed, we discovered that the high-altitude pilots couldn't get a flight from Borneo. That would take another three days.

On our seventh day in Nabire we boarded the helicopter at 6am. There was a low weight restriction owing to our planned high landing at over 4000m so we had to throw out all our extra food. Our agent told us they had plenty of food at their base camp. I had no change of clothes, no extra shoes, no tent, and my rope was tossed into the second flight with the Brits. It felt a bit like a one-way trip. We had no Plan B and no choice but to trust the agent.

I was quite anxious leaving everything behind, but also confident we could pull it off. 'We'll get home somehow,' I thought. I was consoled by the thought that we'd be there for only two days, then we'd be off to Bali. Easy, or so I thought. I had a hotel booked and my kitesurfing gear was waiting for me there.

The two pilots had installed a large oxygen bottle to help them breathe, so I was surprised when one of them lifted his oxygen mask and lit a cigarette just after take-off. It's also common knowledge that helicopters need favourable vision to fly, so I was even more horrified when during our hour-long flight we started flying through thick cloud.

As we were speeding towards a pass we popped out of the cloud flying low over the immense 8km-wide open pit of the Freeport mine. We came in fast across a small lake, smashed into the ground and skidded to a stop. The pilots had planned to get out and help us with our gear, but they kept the power on and screamed at us over the noisy helicopter, 'Get out, get out.' Apparently they were worried they'd damaged the skids. We got out and they took off. I was glad to be standing on solid ground and happy that from then on my personal safety was under my own control.

Base Camp was nestled under steep limestone bluffs next to a picturesque mountain tarn. But as he stood next to the destroyed Base Camp kitchen and dining tent, the agent's local guide was looking grim. Food was scattered everywhere, and it looked more like a rubbish tip.

He said, 'Local tribespeople stole everything,' and I shook my head in frustration.

But the sleeping tents were safely hidden nearby among the rocks and I like to concentrate on what we have, instead of not have, so we set them up and found enough spare parts to make a couple of stoves work. We found a small quantity of rice, but little else, so we set about making the camp as comfortable as possible with tarpaulins and barrels to sit on. It was a pleasant afternoon, so Jamie and I set off for a hike to check out the route to the mountain towering above us – it was surrounded by mist. The second load of British climbers still hadn't arrived with our food, but as we were still eager to attempt the mountain that night we baked rice, shaped it into balls and put a dabble of soy sauce on top – lunch when we reached the summit.

When heavy rain set in during the afternoon we tried to sleep in the thin, damp air, but with summit-day excitement surging through our blood, sleep wasn't beneficial.

2am and we were up, a quick breakfast (we had no food) and we were off. This is what I'd refer to as 'sub-optimal', but Jamie had spent US$35,000 and I wasn't about to wait for a miracle from outside. I knew we needed to have a crack while we were here and healthy and the weather was good. We looked at each other over a weak cup of tea, headlights on in the small dark tent. I smiled and said, 'Let's go climb this thing.'

An hour later we reached the wall and the start of the fixed rope. Climbing in situ fixed rope is sometimes worrisome because you never know the quality of the rope or the anchors until after you've climbed them. But I was pleasantly surprised to find good-quality ropes, and the climbing was enjoyable. The limestone corner had lots of features and the rock was dry and grippy, so we could climb under our own power, then slide up our jumar on the rope which acted as a safety net in case we slipped.

After five pitches we scrambled up a scree gully into another corner followed by several more pitches of fantastic climbing while the dawn slowly turned the dark night into day. We were shrouded in a pale mist, not really rain, but not fine either. After three hours on the wall we arrived at the summit ridge, and soon after I was standing, terrified, at the start of the 30m Tyrolean traverse.

I was expecting this. It was comprised of an old rope stretched tightly across a deep void in the ridge. It was as if a 30m-long section of the ridge we were climbing on had fallen away, leaving a gap to cross.

There was a strong wind blowing, and the ropes were encrusted with 10cm of rime ice. There was an old white Adidas shoe wedged between the ropes and a very sharp edge.

I could just make out the other side through the mist and thought the anchors looked okay. Even so, it took huge courage to swing out onto the ropes, 200m above the ground with the wind blasting and ice exploding off the ropes with every metre I gained as I dragged myself across the void . . .

'What could possibly go wrong?' I called back to Jamie as I swung out onto the rope. He didn't reply, he just looked terrified.

Regardless, it went well and none of the disastrous flashes from bad climbing movies eventuated as I thankfully pulled onto the other side. Jamie followed quickly and we continued along the rocky ridge, enveloped in mist. A feeling of remoteness I'd not felt before was accompanying me high up on that remote peak. The long flights, lack of food, unknown backup, almost no chance of rescue and the yet unknown trip home all weighed on my mind. But five hours after leaving Base Camp we stepped together onto the summit, elated to be there.

We signed the visitor's book that was stored in an old dry coffee tin and turned our minds to the descent before the threatening weather became even worse. Three hours later we were back at Base Camp just before the rain set in again. The British had arrived during the day and were looking uncomfortable being so far from a pub, but with a good supply of cigars and cigarettes they were happy to be there. They were to go up the following day with their local guide for their summit attempt. We were worried they would need rescuing and dreaded having to climb the peak again to bring someone down the steep rock. The plan was for them to climb in the morning, then we'd head down to the mine for a quick excursion to the coastal town of Timika and a late dinner. The helicopter was indeed damaged and there was no chance of a pickup.

Jamie and I slept in the following morning after hearing the second summit team leaving at 3am. Later we went for a hike to East Carstensz to check out the old glacier. It was a clear day, but when we couldn't see the climbers we descended back to base camp for a lunch of two crackers and some weak tea. Then it was time for a nap, fingers crossed that the others would be back before too long.

I woke at 3pm and there was still no sign of them, so I packed some water and jogged up to the wall. I found the group in complete disarray, staggering deliriously off the end of the fixed ropes after having had an 11-hour epic just getting to the Tyrolean traverse. The first person across had flipped upside down on the ropes and hung there for 30 minutes, unable to pull himself upright. The local guide had had to go out and push him back while he was screaming, 'Help me Jesus!' Thankfully, they were safely down so I loaded their packs on top of mine and helped them back to base camp.

After an hour's rest Jamie and I shouldered most of their gear, including one whole pack on top of my pack, and headed off in the dark for our pickup at the edge of the mine, two hours down the valley. We arrived at 10pm with the others turning up around midnight. But much to our amazement security guards arrived in their jeep only a few minutes later. Everyone prepared to jump in, but there were negotiations going on with our local guide that didn't appear friendly. We obviously couldn't understand, but we could tell that the tones were argumentative from the guards and pleading from our agent. I said to Jamie, 'Something is not right.'

Then the guards jumped in their jeep and drove off. Apparently, they were going to check out the route. This was going to be an illegal passage through the mine after all. I'd heard about these illegal passages, and it is why I had the equivalent of a local's yearly salary in USD in my pocket. They would put us in mine workers' uniforms and hard hats then drive us through as if we were staff, bribing each security station as required.

After a couple of hours waiting it started to get cold. We were sitting in a swamp under a rocky overhang called the Zebra Wall.

As two of the British were dangerously cold and completely exhausted, we helped them into sleeping bags. The last thing I felt like doing was helping these idiots, especially when I heard that someone from the mine had walked through camp the day before and the British had mouthed off about how we were going to be sneaking out through the mine.

We woke in the morning as more jeeps turned up with medics and also the mine's Indonesian chief of security. They checked us over then told us to camp in a cave just outside the mine. After numerous satellite phone calls, various visits by security and a long day of waiting, I encouraged the two sick-looking Brits to play up their sickness by shivering and complaining about severe headaches (a sign of high-altitude cerebral edema). But nothing helped and we bedded down for the second night without food, hopeful that a pickup might come during the night.

About midnight we were in luck. A jeep turned up and without saying anything loaded us in and drove into the mine. Five minutes later, it stopped at an old, rat-infested shipping container in the middle of a coal pit. They took away the sick Brits, who it turned out got shuttled through the mine to Timika within a few hours. Their acting had worked – for them at least.

By then we were extremely hungry, and I pleaded with the security guards to find us food and water. They turned up three hours later with a fuel container filled with dirty brown water. It had been three days since we'd drunk or eaten. I hadn't urinated for 24 hours.

The shipping container had two mattresses on a wire-frame bunk bed. I lay down on the floor, my eyes level with a massive, rat-eaten hole in the mattress. We received various visits the next day from the Indonesian security guys, who were friendly, as well as more medics who checked us out.

It slowly dawned on us that our agent had completely screwed us. The permit he had showed us was, in fact, not for the mine, and the mine would never let us through. We were told that the last group had waited for 12 days and had still not been allowed through, having to walk out over New Zealand Pass, which took another week. Luckily, they had food and money to pay off the locals in several villages inhabited by cannibal tribes.

The sole on the local guide's shoe had fallen off. We had no food, no dry clothes and insufficient money, and the British climber stuck with us was incapable of walking a few hours, let alone for seven days.

Jamie was beside himself. 'I have to get home to do a talk,' he said. 'They are paying me more than this trip cost.'

There wasn't much I could say to reassure him. I was trying every trick in the book, and so was the office back in New Zealand. And I was especially gutted because every day here was one less day to kitesurf in Bali . . .

Meanwhile, the mine workers remained friendly and eventually delivered a small amount of cold cooked rice and water. I'd never been starving before, yet I didn't find it too bad. When you have food and you are hungry it's difficult not to eat it. But when you have no food, and no option to get food, your body seems to accept it and the hunger pains aren't that bad. But the dehydration was a worry as we were still at an altitude of 4000m.

On day four I finally had a bowel movement, but it was full of blood, which was also a worry. Our satellite battery was going flat and we had made no progress. The Canadian and New Zealand High Commissions were apparently trying to negotiate our passage through the mine, our agent was trying to charter another helicopter, and the two British who had made it out were trying to negotiate with the mine and communicate with the embassies.

By the end of day four we heard that our agent had given himself up and been arrested by the Indonesian police. There were no helicopters, and the British climber with us was suffering from high-altitude cerebral edema because he was so dehydrated. His condition was bad, but the mine workers refused to believe us, so Jamie and I decided to try and run through the mine and escape, at least to bring attention to our plight. We sent messages out via the satphone that if no one heard from us we would probably have been arrested by the police. At 2am we loaded our packs and with the aid of our headlamps and full of enthusiasm we walked with confidence into the midst of the mine.

'What could possible go wrong?' I said to Jamie. He just smiled and followed my lead.

After an hour we started seeing the monster trucks up close. These things were incredibly intimidating at over three storeys high, and they were being driven at full speed along the deep muddy roads. We could hardly move on the roads as our feet sank deeply into the mud, threatening to not let go of our hiking boots. We immediately feared for our safety.

At an intersection we tried to wave down a truck. Much to our surprise, one stopped. We struggled up its ladders to the bemused driver, who didn't speak a word of English. We communicated with hand signals and said we wanted to go through the mine. I even waved US$1000 dollars at him (over six months' wages), but he couldn't help.

Then a security guard came on the radio and in English told us to wait there, they would come and help us. We clambered down from the truck and waited as instructed until the guard turned up – and took us back to the container.

It was demoralising, all our hope of an escape vanished. I argued with the guards but it was futile. I knew it was not their call and there was no reason to be angry with them, they were just following their orders. They were still friendly enough but were now threatening to take away the little food and water we had been getting.

After waiting for another two hours without a visit from the medics we decided to go again and took off back into the mine. We knew we'd not escape, but we wanted to make sure our frustrations were getting through to the bosses. This time we were surrounded quickly by the security trucks, who were waiting, but the medics also turned up. They took one look at the British climber and took him away.

The following day we were given bottled water, which was unimaginably tasty, so after a couple of hours we were all peeing clear and feeling much better. We were also given boxes of packed lunches with hot rice and chicken wings. We ate everything except the bones. But the message was still the same – we could never pass through the mine.

On the morning of day six the security guards arrived early and said there might be good news. The 'Big Banana' was coming to talk to us. The Big Banana turned out to be a 2m-tall obese ex-US Marine, who pranced around as though he was controlling the Iraq War. I could tell by his demeanour and body shape that he was lazy and autocratic. We had to play this carefully. I smiled and tried to be humble and friendly, taking his side that no, we shouldn't be there, but our agent had screwed us.

His thick southern drawl and patronising language chewed at my patience, but I waited. I did not want to beg him to take us out. He told us how the last group had failed because when he arrived they got angry and threatened him with violence. I just smiled and looked at the ground, waiting.

Eventually he said, 'You wanna get out of here?' Then he shouted, 'Then hurry up and get your gear!'

How quickly a situation can change. Within 10 minutes we were driving through the mine and an hour later we were riding 1000m down the mine's aerial tram and into the Marine's office. We provided statements about what our agent had promised us, and they bought us hot fries and cokes and generally pampered us. All the time they were saying that they might have to send us back to the container, or that the police wanted to arrest us. We were jittery, but a few hours later we were in another jeep heading down to Timika. Another stop, another interrogation by another ex-US Marine, then we surprisingly ended up at the Sheraton Hotel with hot showers and the most amazing buffet I'd ever set eyes on.

We were having dinner when the Big Banana turned up uninvited and sat with us. The British had been there for days and quickly became drunk and started mouthing off about things they shouldn't have been talking so loudly about. The Big Banana told us we couldn't leave the island because the police wanted to arrest us, but our agent was adamant we had to fly out the next morning. Who to believe? We went to the bar, but the Marine turned up there too. As he grilled us for information, he was dropping lines straight out of press releases in the media in Canada and New Zealand, like 'Canadian climber trapped and starved'.

In the morning we got up and went nervously to the airport. After we'd gone through security, we were in the departure lounge when the Marine turned up again. He tapped me firmly on the shoulder so that I turned towards him, then while he was standing confrontationally close, he held his switch-blade knife at my eye level, opened and closed it while he repeated several times, 'Don't leave! Don't get on that plane! The police are coming to arrest you!'

The boarding call came at that moment. I had the Marine towering over me with his knife in my face saying don't go, while a 1.2m-tall Indonesian guy was standing behind me.

'Get on the plane,' he whispered.

I hesitated for a minute, then smiled and turned away from the Marine to walk onto the runway and up the stairs onto the plane. With our seatbelts on, we waited anxiously for the door to be closed, expecting to be pulled off at any minute by the Indonesian police or mine security. But it didn't happen, the door closed and we took off.

I got to Bali in time for my flight home but with time for only one quick afternoon of kitesurfing. I met Jamie again almost 10 years later at Everest Base Camp. He was still a motivational speaker working in Canada.

I laughed that he must have made a fortune from our Indonesian epic. His reply was that he had been so traumatised by it that he had never told a soul.

20

THRILLS IN THE SOUTHERN OCEAN

I was halfway down a 40-degree ski descent, occasionally gazing out over the deep-blue ocean where icebergs were floating, seals were sleeping on the beach, penguins were walking about the snow on the shore and our 20m yacht was anchored in the bay. I smiled to myself. I had returned to the Antarctic Peninsula for my second expedition and this one suited me perfectly – we were just here to ski.

It was then that I started a small avalanche, which a member of our group skied into before being pushed down the slope towards the cold ocean and out of sight around the corner.

'Stop,' I yelled to the others above as I took stock of what had happened . . .

I'd dreamed of going to Antarctica for even longer than I'd dreamed of the Himalayas. Initially I thought the only way was to work for the government at Scott Base, so I set about getting my guiding qualifications so that I could apply for a job. I then found out about the skiing and climbing on the Antarctic Peninsula so shelved the Scott Base idea for a few years.

At the Adventure Consultants office I was planning new trips, and Antarctica was high on my interest level. Guy asked me to plan and price an expedition to sail from Argentina to the Antarctic Peninsula. What a dream trip! I'd grown up on the waters of the Hauraki Gulf, and a combination of the ocean and the mountains was very exciting. I was still a junior in the company, so I didn't have high hopes of beating off the other guides for the opportunity.

When we started marketing the trip, it sold well. Before we knew it we'd secured nine clients and a yacht with five crew. Guy and Luis were the first two guides on, so I entered a note in the budget saying 'Mark will work for free', and kept quiet. A few months later, before anything was talked about, Guy asked me to book flights for him, Luis and me.

The memory of the thump and subsequent scratching of solid-blue sea ice on the steel hull of the yacht still sends a shiver down my spine. I was tucked into a small bunk, about level with the -2°C ocean, in the dark of the short Antarctic summer night, with clothes packed around me so that I couldn't be thrown from my bunk. With my imagination running riot, visualising the ice gouging a hole in the yacht's hull, it was difficult to sleep.

A couple of weeks before, 17 of us had left the Argentine city of Ushuaia, on the 27m Kiwi-owned twin-engine sailing vessel called the *Evohe*. The boat was packed with food, wine and supplies for a 30-day climbing and skiing expedition. The aim was to make first ascents, check out the wildlife, explore 'off the map' and generally have a good time. But first we had to tackle Drake Passage, the body of water between the southern tip of South America at Cape Horn (which is in Chile) and the South Shetland Islands of Antarctica. The passage forms part of the Southern Ocean and is named after the 16th-century English privateer Sir Francis Drake, although he never sailed the passage.

The Drake has earned a place in history as having some of the roughest ocean weather on the planet. It occurs where the fast-flowing Southern Ocean is squeezed between the continental land masses of South America and Antarctica. Storms frequently whip the ocean into a dark-grey, turbulent, heaving mass of water, renowned for sinking many a ship.

Eager with anticipation, we headed out into the Drake on a sunny afternoon in light winds. And that's the way it stayed for the entire five-day crossing – we motored in almost calm conditions.

The colours of Antarctica are mesmerising, even now after more than a dozen expeditions. The water is a deep, cold, blue, with cool white icebergs that change colour depending on the time of day, the cloud cover and the height of the sun. The mountains are a mixture of perfect white with deep, dark slashes across them formed by the thousands of deep bottomless crevasses. Brown and black rocks and towering cliffs protrude from the snow and often leave a scattering of smaller rocks below them as they crumble.

There are a number of good maps of the main shipping channels, used by the boats servicing the numerous bases and cruise ships as well as by the Argentine and Chilean military warships that patrol the waters. Both countries are staking claims to the land in the hope that when the Antarctic Treaty runs out in 15 years or so, they will get valuable land. Probably for mining. They even take pregnant woman there. They give birth on the bases, on the land they are claiming, to give their claims more validity.

The trip went well, even though some of the clients complained about the lack of 'hard' climbing. After four weeks we sailed back to South America with a 10m following sea and a much more exciting Drake Passage.

My next trip to Antarctica was four years later on a more modern but smaller yacht, the 20m *Santa Maria Australis*. We set sail from Ushuaia again and after four full days at sea we spotted land – magnificent glacier-covered mountains cascading into the sea, rich deep-blue oceans, the odd fur seal popping its curious head up, schools of penguins, humpback whales and, most importantly this time, exciting-looking ski slopes.

The skiing in Antarctica is always a challenge. Picking out ice-cliffs and crevasses is especially challenging in bad visibility, so being out front I had to take care skiing first as we picked our way down the nice corn ski runs, making as many turns as possible. We didn't come here to sit about, so we would usually try and ski in all sorts of weather. But as the cloud continued to grow denser during our first day skiing, we decided to carry on back to the yacht, happy to have enjoyed some great turns.

Trying to find the right words to explain the allure Antarctica holds over me, and anyone I take there, is difficult. It's a package deal. It's not just the skiing, it's the remoteness, it's the wildlife, the mountains, the ocean, the grandeur of it, it's as if you are in a giant Cinemax movie. Everywhere you look is spellbinding. The danger is another allure, although guides go to great lengths to minimise it. The crevasses are huge and if you fell into one it might well be fatal. If you twist or break your leg, rescue is extremely difficult and may be impossible. We always ski with extra caution. You know in the back of your mind that if you blow this and break your leg it might well take the yacht a week to get back to Argentina.

As the weather was wet the following day, we headed south through the Lemaire Channel, also known as Kodak Alley because of its steep-sided mountains. They plummet almost vertically into the 100m-wide passage, which is clogged with icebergs and sunbathing seals. The rain had eased by the time we'd tied up at Hovgaard Island, so we went to a nearby penguin rookery and took a few hundred photos of the cute but extremely foul-smelling little critters.

The next day was clear, but a strong southerly wind was blowing and cloud surrounded the summit of Mt Demaria, which we intended to ski. Nevertheless, it wasn't enough to deter our group and we headed over to give it a crack. The one seal we disturbed on the beach looked confused and curious as we unloaded our skis and three-day rescue cache (in case the weather changed and blew up a swell or pushed in brash ice that stopped us getting back to the yacht).

Off we went in improving weather, up the steep, soft snow. It was hard work breaking trail and hot in the Antarctic sun. We were also in the runout of avalanches from above, so for the first two hours we didn't stop, climbing high up above the icebergs floating lazily in Waddington Bay to a shoulder 150m from the cloud-covered summit. What to do? Up or down?

Up of course! Because it was too steep for a skin track, we attached our skis onto our packs and plugged steps up through a rock band and more soft snow to the lovely corniced summit just as the cloud cleared. What a view. We could see the nearby Lemaire Channel with perfect reflections of peaks in its deep blue waters, giant icebergs sunbathing silently in the bay below with occasional seals sleeping on them, inland to the high peaks and the spine of the Antarctic Peninsula with its perfect untouched white ridges, valleys and peaks.

You'd have to call the skiing variable, some good corn, some way too soft. Corn snow is an enjoyable form of skiing. It starts the day frozen ice and ends up as slush. The time in between these two forms is called corn, a very easy and enjoyable form of snow to ski on. But we weren't just there for the turns, it was a smorgasbord of views and sensations. We were close to the bottom when I set off an avalanche that headed towards Nat. Once everyone had stopped, I skied around the corner to see where he'd ended up and found him tucked safely under a rock. No big epic, that was to come later while we were sailing home.

It was a fantastic day and the following one we attempted Mt Scott, but when the 1m ocean surge prevented us from getting ashore, we turned our attention to the smaller but more sheltered Hovgaard Island. We skied four aspects of the 250m-high mountain on near perfect corn completing a good 1000m vertical day.

As we explored northwards towards Paradise Harbour we had all got used to life on the boat. The clients were a group of friends, they'd all known each other for years. Nat was the ring leader and, as Kiwis do, they all gave each other a ribbing whenever possible. As on many of my trips they have all remained friends. I still remember one client, Geoff, who on a daily basis would turn to me, look me in the eye, shake my hand firmly, and say, 'Thank you Mark!' Like them all, he was just so stoked to be there. There was lots of laughter and everyone jumped when there was cooking to be done, or dishes or sailing duties. It was a fantastic group dynamic compared to when seven random people join an expedition.

Whales swam the channels, fur and crab-eater seals watched us, as we watched them, and schools of cute penguins swam by, jumping out of the water as they swam.

Soon enough it was time to head back across the Drake. As the German skipper Jochen wanted to beat a storm forecast for Cape Horn in five days' time, we took off at full speed and for the first 24 hours everything went well.

Then at 1am on day two we had to shut down one of the two engines when the water pump broke. It was unfixable. Back to sleep, it wasn't too much of an issue, we hoped to still beat the storm.

Then at 3am I awoke to yelling. When I turned on my light I was horrified to see that the yacht was filled with smoke. Fire! I threw on my clothes and rushed upstairs to see Nick monitoring the diesel fire which had blown out. No fire thankfully — just smoke.

But then when we looked on deck the skipper and the first mate were holding on for dear life to the end of the mast's steel forward stay with the jib sail pulling roughly on it. It had broken off the deck and was swinging wildly like an angry serpent. The heavy rigging was easily capable of killing someone or smashing the boat if it worked its way free. Victor and I tied into our lifejackets and went to help. They had managed to tie the jib off temporarily, but the sail was still pulling roughly against it. Being out on the deck at night, in the Southern Ocean, in ginormous 15-20m-high rolling swells with a strong wind was extremely intimidating. It took the skipper several dangerous trips up the mast before he managed to retrieve the sail by swinging out and sliding down it with a large sharp knife, cutting the sail away from the steel rigging.

The yacht tipped aggressively to starboard as the swell hit us beam on and while we pitched steeply over there was enough light to see the dark black ocean as it appeared to be pouring off the sides of the Earth and into the darkness. I held on to the mast, also tied in, but the view didn't actually terrify me, it more intrigued me. I was afraid for Jochen because when we lifted him aloft, the moving yacht would throw him into the mast and I'm sure he took quite a beating. It would have been so easy for a loose steel shackle or a sail end to hit someone in the face or head and do some real damage.

That took almost four hours and then the sun started to rise, revealing the major structural support of the mast gone. We were now down to just the one motor, at half speed. By then we were heading directly into the storm.

'What could possibly go wrong?' I asked Victor quietly.

We made a bee-line for Cape Horn, no one speaking aloud about what we'd do if the last engine broke down. We weren't going to sink, but we might have floated extremely uncomfortably around the Southern Ocean for a week until the Argentine or Chilean navy came to rescue us. The group's laughter became more forced and we all sat around much more quietly, waiting for what Cape Horn, with its 800 sunken ships causing the deaths of over 10,000 seamen, would throw at us.

'Worry is a wasted emotion,' I said to Victor as we lay around in our bunks.

But thankfully the storm weakened, and the engine worked tirelessly. After three more tense days we passed Cape Horn in calm, smooth seas accompanied by a large school of dolphins. All of us breathing quiet sighs of relief followed by celebratory drinks.

21

FALLING, FALLING

I was 45 when I started worrying that something was out to nail me. It was that year when I stopped saying my favourite line, 'What could possibly go wrong?' Some people would say I was unlucky, I would say I was lucky! My brain aneurysm could have killed me, the Southern Ocean likewise, and the helicopter crash as well. The final hurdle (I hope) was a nasty fall into a bergschrund.

A friend, Will MacQueen, was killed in a crevasse fall in 2003. The snow bridge he was crossing collapsed and he fell 50m into the guts of the glacier and was killed instantly. He was skiing and this was the first accident of this kind to have happened in New Zealand. Skis usually spread your weight over a crevasse bridge, unlike when you are walking, and our maritime snowpack usually supports you. I was very shocked at Will's death; it was the first death of a friend I could remember and he was doing something I could easily have been doing myself.

This and Dave Hiddleston's death a few months later really rocked my world and made me reconsider my climbing ambitions. I did a lot of soul-searching into what I was doing and the risks

I was taking. Why did I do these things? I most definitely didn't want to die, I didn't have a death wish. I wanted to grow old, lose my hair, get a walking stick, even join the bowling club with my old friends. But I also wanted to live! It's not just the places you go to, the unlikely position you find yourself in on the side of a mountain or cliff face. It's often the people you are with. Mountain and adventurous types are people with a passion; they are similar in ways it is difficult to explain. They have that look in their eye you can pick as soon as you meet them – a sense of humour, the comradeship of relying on them if something goes wrong. Planning and watching the weather every day for the right window to chase a wave, a climb or a flight.

I have nothing against any religion, I like parts of them all, except when one of them tries to pressure you into joining them. My god is Mother Earth, my religion is adventure. Without risk there is little reward, without discomfort you don't know what comfort is, without every muscle in your body aching from pushing yourself for days, you don't understand rest. By getting dirty for days, a shower feels so much better. By running out of food and being hungry, you then enjoy food more.

I may accept more risk than a regular person, I don't deny that. But the sports I've done – skiing, mountaineering, big wall climbing, kitesurfing, paragliding, etc – require a lot of practice. I wasn't instantly good at any of them, I had to learn and build up my skills. To a layperson's eye what we do might be thought of as insane, but I do not go into it thinking 'Nothing will happen to me'. I'm always running through worst-case scenarios in my head. 'What if this avalanches? What if the rope cuts? What if the wind increases?' and so on.

I must have a powerful sense of survival, but maybe there are weaknesses elsewhere in my make-up that I'm trying to compensate for. I don't really know, I've never thought about it until writing this. I guess I don't care too much. To me what is important is health and good times with family or friends.

I really don't agree with the cottonwool that society seems to be trying to wrap around everyone. Kids play computer games instead of skateboarding down the neighbourhood road; adults watch rugby while drinking harmful amounts of liquor instead of going for a walk or a run themselves; we all drive to the shop in a rush, instead of walking 15 minutes to it and taking in the view. Then when someone gets hurt or something goes wrong, there has to be someone to blame. We seem to have stopped saying, 'It was an accident'.

It was spring 2015 and a German client had booked me for one-on-one guiding. He said he wanted to do a *lot* of skiing; when clients like that turn up, a lot can mean 500m vertical in a day or 1500m. He was very fit, wanting more like 3000m of vertical and I was fresh out of a winter of heli-skiing, so not overly fit.

We flew into the head of the Tasman Glacier and set about ski touring each day. He pushed me physically and we skied long days. But he was never satisfied, always wanting more and steeper skiing. We'd ski a long run, then after skinning up for an hour he'd say, 'Can we do that again?' – despite it being near dark and me heading for the hut and a cuppa tea. I wasn't comfortable being alone with him, without backup, on steeper mountains. When the occasional client pushes me I usually pride myself in not forcing myself into doing anything dangerous. It's my job as the guide to do that.

We had a good week and did a lot of skiing, but the bad weather was coming in and he didn't want to be stuck sitting around Tasman Saddle hut for a few days. We loaded our gear and skied down the glacier. After dumping all the unnecessary gear, we skinned up the Darwin Glacier to just below Mt Rumdoodle. Its south-east face was a steep snow slope reaching well over 45 degrees, with what looked like a harmless run onto the glacier. So I suggested we climb the face and ski it. The client was stoked and super excited because it looked challenging and was covered in excellent winter snow.

We skinned up towards the face. The slope grew steeper and under the 20cm of cold winter snow it was icy. When our skins started to slip backwards on the ice, it was time to remove our skis and crampon up the slope.

We stopped near each other and I stepped out of one ski. I kicked my ski boot into the ice. It was quite hard, so I kicked my boot harder into the snow. I knew instantly what had happened before I started falling. My kick had fractured the 1m-thick bridge over the bergschrund and it had zippered 30m left of me, 50m right and 10m across. Very unusual for a New Zealand snowpack.

With a quiet 'puff' the entire bridge fell into the bergschrund, with me on it. I grabbed feebly at the snow as I fell silently 10m down into the depths of the crevasse. I had no time for fear or panic, concentrating on staying upright and balanced. Falling with grace, you could call it. The fracture had occurred 20-30cm below my client's feet, so thankfully he stayed put while I fell. He later said, 'You just disappeared'.

It was a long way down and as I hit the bottom I was crushed by blocks of snow landing with solid 'thumps' on top of me and pinning me down. I panicked briefly, struggling to move, but I was held firm. My heart was racing. I knew I was in a terrible position, while my client was left alone on the edge of the cliff I'd fallen off. I forced myself to breathe deeply and relax. I was not dead, I could breathe and fighting would not help. I forced the panic down inside me, which allowed me to think.

It wasn't dark. I could see light through the blocks of snow and my lower legs seemed free. I pushed at the blocks with my bare hands (it had been hot on the surface so I wasn't wearing any gloves). One moved, but I was on the verge of panic again and forced myself to lie still for a minute. *I will live,* I thought. *Just conserve your energy.*

I had another go at moving the blocks and managed to push a few away. I was cutting my bare hands on the sharp snow as I made a tunnel out to the light. After a few minutes I was able to dig myself out and crawl on top of the blocks. I called out to my client to say I was okay. He replied that he was just about to set off my emergency locator beacon (EPERB), which I had given him to carry. I told him not to move and climbed over to the side wall of the crevasse.

I left all my gear there as I was in a panic to get out of the deep, dark hole in the glacier. The wall to the surface was about 4m high and I'd left my ice axe and crampons in my pack where I'd been buried.

I was desperate to set eyes on my client because if he slipped it was a 10m fall into the bergschrund. I punched the fingertips of my bare hands into the icy wall of the bergschrund, kicked my feet in and scampered up the wall onto the surface of the glacier and into the sunshine.

I felt better instantly, especially when I saw the client patiently waiting. I looked to the left and with an exhale of air as if I'd been kicked in the guts I realised I was looking over at the bergschrund on Mt Green a few kilometres away where I had been buried by an avalanche in 1995.

After several deep breaths and a discussion, we decided it was best if he put on his crampons and climbed away from the bergschrund to a spot higher up where he could put on his skis. I felt pretty helpless, but with no skis and no gear there wasn't much I could do.

I watched him meticulously, coaching him to a safe spot where he changed into his skis, skied around to the side of the bergschrund and hiked up to my position. Once I was satisfied that he was safe I had to climb back into the bergschrund to get my gear. That went fine; I downclimbed the 4m wall to stand on the debris that had fallen in with me, then carefully walked over to where I'd been buried. I retrieved all my gear, except one ski pole, and climbed back out. This time I put my spare gloves on and climbed back out of the crevasse.

My only injury from the 10m fall, besides cuts on my hands and hurt pride, was a broken thumb nail. Whew! I was lucky again! But I felt stupid to have fallen into the crevasse. I should have known it was there, I should have stopped earlier to put the crampons and rope on, I should not have even gone up that slope. I've always said it's not bad to make mistakes as a guide, but to admit them early and alter your decisions is the right way forward. I got the satphone out and called the Adventure Consultants office, asking them to pass on the word to all the other guiding companies about the dangerous snow bridges and for other guides to be careful.

We decided to ski down the glacier and catch our flight back to Aoraki/Mt Cook Village for a shower and a beer. Over the next few days he didn't push me again to ski steeper or more vertical. His only comment was, 'I thought I'd lost you, Mark'. But my job as the guide was to absorb that pressure and make the right decisions. What happened was not his fault.

Another time I got pushed by a group of Russian clients while heli-skiing in Kashmir. We'd told them about the dangerous avalanche conditions before we took their money. 'We can only ski low-angle runs,' I'd said, and they'd said that was fine.

But after the first run they all said, 'We want steeper,' in thick Russian accents and again on the second run, 'We want steeper'. By the bottom of the third run I'd placed my earmuffs on my head as if the helicopter was approaching. They got frustrated, then angry by my refusal to listen. I just smiled, and by the fourth run they were laughing and joking with me. The day ended well and there was even a decent cash tip!

22

TO THE END OF THE EARTH

600km from the South Pole is Scott Glacier. On this particular day the radio crackled into life. It was Leo with panic in his voice.

'My pulk's in a crevasse and it's pulling me towards it. Help!'

It was the call I'd been dreading.

A pulk is a long sled in which you load all your gear and tow it behind you. Our pulk was full of climbing and camping gear, kites and enough food for 70 days in Antarctica.

Weighing nearly 200kg each, they were easy enough to pull behind us across the ice with a kite. But for a person swinging below in free space, they were literally a deadweight . . .

Leo was a professional climber and adventurer from Britain. He'd been speaking at our Mountain Film Festival in Wanaka. We were catching up over a beer when he received a phone call. It was bad news. The third member of his team, bound for a kiting and climbing expedition to Antarctica, had had to pull out. His father had terminal cancer and he needed to spend time with him.

'Where can I possibly find someone who can kite, ski, climb, take two months off without pay, has Antarctic experience, photography and cinematography skills, and can join me at such short notice?' he asked.

Coincidentally I was returning from guiding a ski tour on the Antarctic Peninsula to Ushuaia, Argentina, just a few hours' bus ride from their team's meeting point in Chile, on the day their trip started.

'I can,' I said casually, not expecting him to take me seriously. He gave me an appraising look.

'You're in,' was all he said.

I suggested he went home to find someone younger and fitter. We really didn't know each other well, although I think I can tell quite quickly when I meet someone if I'll get along with them. It's the look in their eye, a passing comment, an attitude. I'm not sure exactly what, although I still thought he'd find someone better suited than me. After all, it was only three years since I had broken my back in the helicopter accident. I'd never tested any of their gear (they'd been training for five years). I'd never towed a pulk with a kite. I hadn't been doing any rock climbing for over a decade and they were 12 to 13 years younger than me. Both were professional climbers.

When Leo called in early August and once again asked me to join him, I told him I'd need a few days to decide. During seven sleepless nights, one night I'd think I'd go then the next I'd wake in a panic and decide to flag it. Then I'd think, could I keep up? Would I enjoy it? Did I want to put myself through it? Would my back handle it?

What could possibly go wrong?

On day seven Jo asked me if I was going. I explained my concerns, but her reply was simple.

'You can't not go. You've been training for this trip all your life.' Which was true, I'd been kitesurfing and kiteskiing for 15 years, whereas Leo had just learnt especially for the trip. Jean was very accomplished. I'd skied professionally, ski patrolling and guiding for 20 years, and although Leo was a good skier, he was not at the same level as me.

I also had the electronic skills to manage all the cameras and computers, more medical skills and general mountaineering experience than either of them and more cold-weather experience too. Jo made me realise I wouldn't need carrying along; some of the time I'd be leading – and I'd have a lot to contribute.

I called Leo and told him I was in. As it turned out, I was the most relaxed of the group much of the time, although I was the weak link physically. Some days, after nine or 10 hours on the go, I'd call via the radio and explain that I was tired and needed to stop. Jean would sometimes say he was not tired, so why should we stop? That usually didn't sit well with me, but Leo was always the diplomat and we'd come to a compromise and usually stop. At which time Leo would often also confess he was shattered and happy to stop.

In early November 2017 we flew from Punta Arenas in Chile to Antarctica on a chartered Russian Ilyushin jet, which landed at Union Glacier Camp on a blue-ice runway. We shared the flight mostly with Seven Summit climbers heading to the highest mountain in Antarctica, Vinson Massif, a peak I'd climbed five times. I'd had some laughs on this flight before.

The Ilyushin jet is a Russian cargo plane first built in 1971 – without windows. Behind us, piled to the roof, were fuel containers and food for the base. There was a Russian crew member sitting in the back with us, a navigator downstairs at the front and five pilots upstairs in the cockpit. They all looked sober, but typically Russian and very sombre.

The crew member with us stood up and started a typical safety demonstration – seatbelts, emergency exits and so on. Then after mentioning the life jackets under our seats he started laughing.

'The water is minus two,' he said through tears of laughter. We too laughed –uncomfortably.

During the flight I'd squeezed through the narrow passage to the navigator's pod at the front of the plane for a look. It was a glass bubble of windows. A Russian guy was sitting there looking concerned as he stared blankly at a wall of complicated instruments. Out of the window I could see ocean and ice as we flew south to the massive continent of Antarctica. I smiled and said hi over the roar of the jets. He smiled at me and I nodded at the instruments.

'Impressive,' I said, whereupon he shook his head and pulled out a hand-held Garmin GPS valued at $250.

'All broken,' he said, pointing to the device in his hand as if that was what he was using to navigate.

We landed on white ice but with no windows I could hardly tell when the wheels touched down. The engine sound diminished and I felt a gentle bump, then the roar of the engines when they were thrown into reverse as we slowly decelerated over 8-10km. Eventually the plane stopped and we piled on our warm gear, down pants and jackets before stepping into the frigid air of inland Antarctica. The ice was so polished from a millennium of Antarctic winds that we could hardly stand upright as we stepped off the plane into a fresh -15°C.

The three of us were heading on the adventure of a lifetime – a 10-week, almost 2000km kiteskiing and man-hauling expedition to climb the Spectre, one of the most remote mountains on Earth. The trip cost US$350,000, with a prepaid rescue bond of US$100,000 on top – all of which Leo had raised through his sponsors and supporters. Even so, we had to economise. If we'd had another US$100,000 we could have flown to the mountain, but we didn't, so our plan was to use kites to pull us the last 400km there and then all the way back to Union Glacier.

We spent a few days sorting food and repacking gear, and it was then that I learnt why Leo's nickname was Captain Faff. I'd never heard of the word faff, but it means *spend time in ineffectual activity*. And boy did we do that. We'd unpack something, look at it, talk about it, then instead of packing it, place it aside to talk about it more later. I was gobsmacked. As a guide you do all this stuff really quickly so that you can finish the job and have a beer.

But it was fun, and I enjoyed ribbing the guys about it as we started building a great relationship full of jokes and laughter. I remember when we split up the gear and I said I'd carry the 55l of fuel, which I estimated weighed 55kg. Once all the pulks were packed we did a weigh-in and for some reason my pulk was significantly lighter than the other two. It took some working out, but it turned out that fuel weighs quite a lot less than water. Jean never trusted me again after that and ribbed me for days.

On 20 November ALE (the logistics company that supports expeditions to Antarctica) told us we'd be flown out in five hours and to make sure we were ready. The ALE owners and employees are great guys, and most adventures in Antarctica have been possible only because of their support and their operation. I knew them quite well from my five Vinson expeditions and they treated us like rock stars.

We loaded our 200kg pulks into the Twin Otter to fly as far towards our goal as we could get. As we took off I switched between in control and moments of sheer panic. I'd sweat and shake, wondering what the hell I was doing. Maybe these guys were crazy and wanted someone to push into a crevasse to make their story sound better? But that was crazy thinking and I had to control my imagination. I could see from looking at them they were going through similar moments of panic, two months without their young kids, can we do it? Will we need rescuing? We joked lightly with each other, but there was no doubting the magnitude of the expedition ahead of us. What had Leo got us into?

We took off towards the South Pole, flying kilometre after kilometre over massive glaciers and wide-open crevasses. The distance we had to cover was enormous and daunting. But first we made a four-hour flight to what must be the most remote gas station in the world. Thule Corner consisted of nothing more than several barrels of aviation fuel buried in the snow and a toilet block.

'Nothing is easy down here,' said our pilot in a thick Canadian accent, as he bashed at the frozen fuel cap on a barrel with a steel wrench in an attempt to open it. His voice stuck with us and we would repeat his phrase almost daily on our journey ahead.

We flew onwards with the pilot taking us close to 'the point of no return' where he had to turn back or risk running out of fuel. There he set us down on bumpy hardpack. We were 3000m above sea level and 200km from the South Pole. The cold smacked us in the face as we disembarked. It was -35°C, with 10 to 15 knots of wind. It was galling to contemplate the months of that – and doubtless worse – that lay ahead. We had to steel ourselves not to turn around and get back on board. Jean would humorously mimic exiting the plane doors and freezing solid with an 'irk'. But we'd expected this and I welcomed it.

We unloaded the plane before the pilot waved goodbye and flew back to the comforts of Union Glacier. I had to fight down the urge to panic as the sense of isolation and the magnitude of the journey sank in. I had still not even tried out my ski boots, and I didn't even know if I'd move at all once I was tied to my 200kg pulk.

As we set up the tent in the bitter cold, I noticed clouds on the horizon.

'Looks like a storm brewing,' I said. The others looked at me as if I was nuts. Apart from the wispy clouds on the horizon, the blue was near perfect. I was blown away by the beauty and serenity of the Polar Plateau, the white snow surface etched out by wind into small wave-like formations, dotted by occasional sastrugi scattered like cacti in the desert. Sastrugi are features formed by the erosion of snow by wind and are up to a metre high. The distant horizon looked curved like the edge of the Earth and met the deep blue sky – except in the one direction where the clouds were brewing. As you walked around, the snow surface squeaked loudly under the rubber of our overboots. The cold forced us into our tents, where we ended up cooking dinner and talking about the trip ahead.

I woke during the night to a full-blown Antarctic storm as 40-knot gusts drove snow horizontally into our tent walls. That was weird. The Polar Plateau is a desert and it barely snows all year.

After breakfast we went outside to check on the tent and gear and shoot some footage for the movie we were making about our trip. Filming with down mittens in temperatures approaching -60°C with wind chill was not much fun, but we kept our spirits up with jokes and banter. 'This was not in the brochure,' I said to Leo, and Jean agreed. It was, once again, a good occasion to get to know each other. We laughed, even though all of us understood the precariousness of our situation. A stove flare-up could melt our tent or a gust of wind could rip it apart, and we wouldn't survive for long. Our tent was a fragile cocoon, like a lunar capsule, protecting us from certain death in the intensely hostile atmosphere outside.

On day five the clouds parted and the winds eased to 20-25 knots. In bitter cold we rigged up our 9m Ozone kites. We knew that we'd be overpowered, but they were the smallest we had. We presumed that the heavy pulks would need a fair bit of power to get moving. We had 8m traces on them, so if we crashed the pulk would hopefully stop, or at least slow down, before running us over like a speed bump. We also tied knots in the rope, a standard glacier travel technique, so that if a pulk fell into a crevasse, the knot might catch in the snow and not pull us in with it.

So with our pulks tied to us, lines laid out and untangled, kites held down with blocks of snow, we'd be ready. A nervous pull on the front lines would wake up the kite and send it skywards, sometimes also lifting us off the snow until the rope to the pulk held us firm. Once we'd gained control, we'd put the kite in the direction we wanted to go and it would drag us and the pulks across the snow. It was like sailing on a solid surface.

Jean launched first while I filmed. He was immediately hoisted several metres off the ground before he got the kite under control. Leo went next and was hoisted even higher.

We kited for three to four hours that first day, moving quickly over the rough snow, sometimes encountering metre-high sastrugi. A flipped pulk meant sidestepping or kiting back to right it. Because we were so overpowered this wasn't easy because the kite was always trying to drag us in the opposite direction. However, I was so stoked that we could move with our heavy loads, and I looked back often to check that the pulk was still there. The system for pulling the kite allowed for very little pressure on our bodies – we were kind of floating in the middle.

We still had much to learn. After a while my goggles froze, reducing my vision to a blurry haze. It was critical that no skin be exposed to the elements as it would freeze in a minute or less, signalling frostbite and the end of the expedition. I called up and told the others I had to stop, and ejected my kite. Unfortunately the others were in the same position and we ended up 500m apart. This caused us to spend over an hour dragging the pulks together into what became a hastily convened camp. Even so, we were stoked to be moving after the storm.

The next morning as I fumbled with my camera in heavy down mittens filming the guys launch their kites, I somehow accidently hit the format button, then the confirm button. My eyes were watering in the cold and I could barely believe what I'd done. *Fuck!* I was so gutted to see the filming from our first day being formatted over. I'd lost it all. I made sure to take more care with what I was doing.

From then on, we covered as much ground as we could each day. The winds were stronger than we'd anticipated. We'd been told about polar high-pressure systems that gave clear skies and 10-12 knot winds. But we were battling 20-plus knots and stormy skies.

We'd kite for as long as possible before having to eject our kites because the excessive power meant holding on any longer would result in an injury. We'd erect our camp and crawl into our tents out of the wind. The kite had a safety system, so that when you ejected it the pulling force was mostly gone and the kite just flapped on one line, still connected to a backup safety system. But it meant that the kite lines were in a terrible tangle. Every day we'd set out with high hopes, but every evening we'd crawl, completely spent, into our tents. It became known as the 'Spectre spanking'.

'Nothing was easy,' as the man said.

We wore 8000m down suits to keep our bodies warm, but despite ski boots three sizes too large, lined with special liners and a neoprene overboot, our feet often became too cold. Frostbite was a real concern.

'I can't feel my toes,' said Jean one morning. Almost immediately I put his bare feet on my stomach for 30 minutes to warm them up. Leo joked about my ample belly being a great toe warmer. I joked later that my butt crack was a perfect warmer for his frostbitten nose! Bare skin would freeze so swiftly and if you removed your goggles you could feel the liquid in your eyes freezing over between blinks.

Part of Leo's expedition plan was to find the Americans' South Pole Highway. This road travels from the Ross Ice Shelf to the South Pole. The Americans drag millions of gallons of kerosene along it to fuel their base at the South Pole. The route is marked and they check it with sonar, filling in any crevasses with huge earth movers as they go. We found the road on day three, but the convoy hadn't been through that summer and it was well drifted over. But the flags every 300m made navigation easy. Our plan was to follow that road for about 150km before turning off and descending the Polar Plateau to the mountains.

After a few hours following the road we were surprised to see a convoy coming towards us, materialising out of the white. They were more than likely surprised to see three kiteskiers travelling from the South Pole, especially so early in the season. The convoy looked like a scene out of a Mad Max film – diggers, snow groomers, accommodation containers, skidoos and a dozen workers. Jean stopped briefly to chat to them, while I shot some photos and film, all the time holding onto my feisty kite pulling on me in the strong winds. Then we carried on north.

The 20m-wide, perfectly groomed piste they had left behind was indeed special. It was smooth and fast and relatively easy kiting. It was especially pleasant as we were travelling through an area known as the Sastrugi National Park. We blasted down the road until the wind overpowered us and we had to eject the kites.

That was the point where we intended to turn off the road and head for the mountains. It was where we buried our second cache with food, fuel, whiskey and some treats like a meal of frozen pre-cut chicken, vegetables, noodles and a satay sauce (my addition to the meal plan). The first cache had been at our drop-off point with food, fuel, treats and Christmas presents.

It was on day eight that things really spiced up. We were kiting from the Polar Plateau, slowly losing height, when the terrain in front of us dropped out of sight. The surface turned to concrete-hard blue ice with car-sized ridges and truck-swallowing crevasses. I had an idea of what was ahead and called Leo on the radio to say we must be off route, because it looked like an icefall. The wind was strong, over 25 knots, and we couldn't stop the kites lifting us off the ground if we flew them overhead. He replied that the GPS route we had was pointing that way.

We carried on. I was last man and came over a bulge to see Leo's pulk upturned below him with the trace stuck around an ice bulge. Jean was trying to get to Leo's pulk to flip it upright. But his own kite and pulk were also downwind and downhill of him, threatening to drag him down the icefall.

All we could do was eject our kites and roll them up so we could then right the pulks. The pulk skids were failing to gain traction on the ice and were sliding below us sideways, scraping loudly across the blue ice. We skied them down gingerly, all the while on the verge of being dragged into a potentially deadly headlong tumble down the icefall. By the time we reached the bottom intact, we found more blue ice and it took us a further two hours to find a patch of snow to camp on. There we stayed for two days, waiting out the strong winds. Luckily we'd dropped 1500m and the temperature had risen to -20°C – without the wind it seemed relatively warm.

By day nine I was starting to worry about our slow progress. We'd expected to reach the mountain in less than a week, but at this rate it would take much longer. Earlier Leo had been struggling with the scale of the expedition and I think I helped by telling him we just had to live in the moment, enjoy each day and only worry about the immediate problems. It was the mindset that helped me climb many big mountains, such as Mt Everest. One step at a time. Then I asked Leo if he was worried about how long it was taking to get to the Spectre.

'Hell no, this is just the sort of adventure I wanted,' he said with a smile. He was loving it, and so was I. I'd already developed a huge amount of respect and admiration for Leo, and that comment added to it. His attitude throughout the entire expedition made the trip for me, and he always dispelled any bickering or inclination to argue straightaway.

When the wind dropped on day 10, we relaunched our kites cautiously – we hadn't even taken the 12 or 15m kites from their bags – and had our first enjoyable kite session. We had reached the Californian Plateau, close to the mountains. It had smooth-powder fields and was crevasse-free. We were relishing high-speed downwind travel, for a while . . .

A few hours later we were overpowered again, on hard-white ice in the middle of the extremely crevassed Scott Glacier. As I was dragging my pulk to our intended camp, a snow bridge over a hidden crevasse collapsed as my pulk softly nudged it. Jean went back and while I filmed he slapped the snow surface over a crevasse with his hand. A huge piece of it fell into the depths of the glacier. Gulp! We'd kited over hundreds of those earlier that day.

Kiting there was clearly foolhardy, so the next day we roped together while towing our pulks for six hours of hard walking over ice bulges and around dangerous crevasse bridges to get to where we could kite again.

'We're getting spanked,' wrote Leo on the daily blog. 'Nothing is easy down here!'

It was day 16, and we were only one kilometre short of the Spectre when I went ahead to set up the much-anticipated arrival shot. But disaster struck when Leo's pulk fell through a snow bridge into a crevasse and dragged him toward it. One minute he was kiting towards the mountain, the next he was flying through the air backwards towards the crevasse. Luckily the knots we'd placed in the rope caught on the lip and he stopped. Too scared to move, he lay there and waited for help. Jean ejected his kite and without concern for his own safety ran over the snow to him. He quickly screwed in an ice screw and clipped Leo to it, which stopped him being dragged into the crevasse.

It had all happened in a few seconds and it really could have been all over in those few seconds. Leo may well have been killed if that knot hadn't caught. After some man hugs and a few minutes backing up the ice screw with another one, Jean abseiled into the crevasse and laboriously emptied the pulk, while hanging in space so they could pull up the heavier items separately before hauling out the pulk.

We set up camp below the impressive 1000m granite faces, then after a few days exploring the different aspects of the mountain, we set off to climb it via the only established route. It had only been visited and climbed once before — 40 years ago, by the famous American climber Mugs Stump and his geologist brother Ed. They landed a plane on the Californian Plateau and drove down on a skidoo reportedly well stocked with lobster tail and LSD.

We set off at 8am and after climbing a steep snow couloir, we moved on to the rocky upper-north face. It was steep, perfect-pink granite with very few cracks – just chimneys and off-widths. Jean and Leo are both world-class climbers, which showed as they led pitch after pitch of tricky mixed climbing. We were not on the Stump Route, that was for certain! The climbing was much harder than what was possible in the 1980s. Weight constraints meant we only had super-light alloy ski-touring ice axes and lightweight-hybrid crampons, designed for approaches and glacier skiing. Hardly an ideal setup.

After 15 hours of difficult and dangerous climbing in deteriorating weather, it was 11pm – for once the ever-constant sun was blocked out by the clouds – when we clambered onto the summit. It was a little bittersweet, as we didn't really feel like celebrating. We felt completely strung out. So alone and isolated. We were the most remote humans on Earth at that moment. So very far from home – and not even sure if we could get off the mountain let alone get home.

We'd climbed up in a corkscrew direction, meaning as we climbed higher we kept climbing left, over unknown terrain, so it was potentially dangerous to abseil that way. The weather had been getting worse all day and we hadn't even brought our down jackets with us. We could see our camp way down below and our descent route was unknown. But we were stoked to be there and maybe the anxiety overran the satisfaction a little. I think at that time we didn't realise this would be the only time we would climb the mountain.

We took some quick photos and made a hasty retreat. Seven rappels later we regained our camp at 5am after 21 hours on the go. Within 30 minutes a storm blew in and buffeted our camp. We'd done well to avoid it. Stuck on that mountain in high winds would have quickly become an epic attempt at survival.

We spent the next week trying the different surrounding peaks – all unclimbed – but it wasn't meant to be. We kept getting shut down by severe winds and unsettled weather. We managed to climb only one more before it was time to set off on our 1400km journey back to Union Glacier and our flight home.

'We can't push too hard,' said Leo. 'Or else I'll be going home to my kids with no toes or fingers.' Jean and I agreed and I personally felt relieved to be setting our sights on home.

First we had to man-haul up the Scott Glacier. Man-hauling means dragging the 150kg pulks for 50 minutes followed by a 10-minute break. It was tiresome, monotonous, hard work for hour after hour, yet many polar explorers do it for week after week. The extreme crevasse nature of the Scott Glacier meant we had to weave around crevasses and over ice bulges with our shoulders straining, calves burning and backs aching. One 10-hour day we made only 12km due to the physical challenges of man-hauling the heavy pulks uphill, over very rough ice and around crevasses.

Jean was navigating and I was concerned he was cutting corners to save time. This caused one of our most heated debates. I wanted to take the longer and less crevassed route that we had come down, while Jean wanted to take the direct route and weave around the crevasses. I was incredibly frustrated but had no choice but to follow. I was working hard to keep up with the guys, my pulk was probably lighter than either of theirs, but I'd strained my Achilles tendon and my back was incredibly sore. I always knew this part was going to be the toughest.

When we followed Jean's shortcut we all too soon found ourselves in trouble. The surface was hard-blue ice, which was easy for towing the pulks, but we had to cross occasional 8-10m-wide sagging snow bridges. We had the rope on, but I was certain that if someone fell in, their weight and their pulk would easily pull us all into the crevasse because the surface was so slippery. We went on hour after hour, crossing more and more soft-snow bridges. Jean's foot would sometimes push through the bridge and he'd backtrack and choose another part to cross. He did an awesome job leading through the nerve-racking crevasses.

It was also very windy and we needed softer snow to camp on. We had used ice screws to secure the tent, but when the wind blew under the tent, it was far less comfortable. We also needed softer snow to melt for water. After a long 12-hour day, after dozens of terrifying crevasse crossings, we spotted a drift of snow in a depression (it wasn't a crevasse), erected our tent and slumped inside out of the wind.

As usual we were good at leaving our frustrations outside at night and we never indulged in revisiting arguments inside the tent. It was that night when we received an email from ALE. They were tracking us via our inReach satellite device and were concerned about where we'd walked and our position. The crevasses could be seen from space and they told us it was an extremely dangerous area. In other words, we shouldn't have been there. Jean never did apologise for that 'shortcut'.

Then on the fifth day of man-hauling, the surface cleaned up, the crevasses thinned out and we broke out our big 15 square-metre kites on extra-long 60m lines. We covered 110km of tacking that day, making 36km upwind towards home. By edging our skis and pulling against the kite we could tack upwind. As a yacht has a keel, we had our legs and skis. It was hard work, but we'd covered more than twice the distance that we could walk in a day. No one had ever done that in Antarctica before and we were elated that it worked with our heavy loads.

From that day on we rested when there was no wind and kited when there was. 100km days became the norm, our speed dependent on the surface conditions. These varied often, sometimes several times in an hour. It could be blue glacier ice, hard-white ice, rough, wind-etched sastrugi, soft powder or a combination of all those.

When we came to our second cache of food and fuel at the American South Pole Highway, there was a wonderful surprise. Leo and Jean had studied the winds on our route over the past five years. It always blew directly from the Pole, in a south-east direction. That is why we had 10 days of food and fuel for the 10-day walk back to our first cache, at the drop-off point.

But the wind was blowing 90 degrees different. It was blowing across the road, not directly down it. No one spoke as we packed the cache into our pulks and launched our kites again, even though it was getting late and we were already tired (well, I was). The convoy had also passed through recently, probably on their way back from the Pole, so we motored along the road, doing close to 50 km/hr. It sounds easy, but all the weight of your body is on the downwind foot, which in turn freezes. That knee also tended to swell and lock up.

We had covered 120km of the 150km road when I had to stop. The guys were gutted, but I was in terrible pain and couldn't go on. I said I'd rather walk the last 30km than sustain an injury. Leo was also stuffed, and once we stopped he was happier. It should have been a day of celebration, and I felt bad having stopped us short of our drop-off point, just because I was tired. I was really disappointed.

Thankfully the next morning the wind was still blowing in the same direction and we kited the final 30km to our drop-off cache. It was nearly Christmas Eve and all of a sudden we'd made up eight days of travel. The wind was still blowing in a strange direction – from the direction we needed to go home. That meant it wasn't possible to kite that way until things changed. The forecast for Christmas Day was a good wind direction, so we celebrated Christmas a day early with a feast of fried sausages, mashed potato, peas and gravy (one of my favourite Antarctic meals), presents and whiskey.

Jean gave us both a pair of clean French boxers. I gave them chocolates from New Zealand and Leo gave us chocolates from the UK. It was a fun, relaxing day. Our Christmas tree was a piece of sastrugi that we cut down and decorated with decorations Leo had brought from home.

I'd visited Leo and Jean in the UK a few months before to help pack the freight, and while I was there I got Leo's wife Jess and daughter Freya to make him a Christmas card. I knew this would be a real tear-jerker for the film and I had the cameras rolling when he opened it and read it. As he read the card the inevitable happened and this hardened explorer wept openly while reading out his daughter and wife's words on the card for the camera. To be honest, I think we all wept.

After we arrived back at our drop-off point it was a mere 1100km to Union Glacier where we'd started. The next week was the most frustrating of the trip with light winds from the wrong direction. We spent two days tacking hard upwind. It was crippling our legs and we were not making enough ground upwind. And the light winds were forcing us towards a heavily crevassed area. We struggled for only a few kilometres each day and in the light winds it was easy to get separated by a few kilometres. Often we became hot as we tried to run upwind, pulling our kites into the sky where the hope of stronger winds lay. Jean was an outstanding kiter and could deal with much lighter winds than me or Leo. Sometimes it fell on him to drag our pulks together at camp when the wind had all but died.

It was terribly hard on our bodies. My downwind foot was dead with cold, and it felt as if it was a wooden stump. That knee was painfully stiff. But once or twice a week there wouldn't be much wind and we'd take an off-day, sitting around and eating, treating ourselves to whiskey or rum in our tea, and just gazing at the wondrous scenery.

I'd always thought the flat Plateau would be boring and monotonous, but it was far from that. While it was flat for as far as you could see, the surface was sculptured and etched by the wind. It's like looking at clouds – your eyes pick out shapes and features. The snow was covered with surface hoar, a flat two-dimensional snow crystal that forms when super-cooled water droplets freeze on the surface. They sparkled in the changing light. If you got down on the snow and looked closely at them, they looked like small feathers or flat ice cream cones. The wind would blow them into piles and you could pick up a handful in a gloved hand (they were -20°C to touch) and let them pour through your fingertips.

The light would change regularly as the sun and the clouds moved, casting shadows at different angles and warming us in the tent. But the sun would also never go down, it would just do large slow circles above us, 24 hours a day. At home I can estimate the time from the height of the sun at different times of the year. Early and later in the day is easiest, but down here there was no reference. The sun looked the same in the afternoon, the night time or the morning.

The flatness wasn't that flat either, or it played tricks on your mind. Sometimes I'd see huge shallow valleys ahead and we'd contour through them like crossing a large lake bed. There would be nothing ahead, then all of a sudden we'd pass a bulge in the snow, like an island in a lake, and a few minutes later it'd be gone. It was a moon-like landscape. Dead and deserted. But also pristine and breathtaking. I felt so damn lucky to be there.

Playing music such as Pink Floyd's 'Wish You Were Here' on my headphones while kiteskiing across this landscape brought for me a feeling of euphoria like no other. It might last for a few hours – until the surface turned to ice or my legs hurt even more – and it was back to fighting for every kilometre. But on the Plateau it was amazing much of the time.

A few days later we were treated to an incredible atmospheric display. The Antarctic air is often loaded with ice crystals and these refracted the sun's light to produce one of the most amazing natural phenomena any of us had ever seen. A 22 degree halo formed around the sun, with double sun dogs (mini-suns sitting on either side of the halo), a sun pillar (a vertical line running through the sun) and a parhelic circle (a horizontal line joining the sun and the sun dogs). All that set off numerous rainbows around the sun and also horizontally around the sky.

'It's the sun dog of my dreams,' shouted Jean as he leapt from the tent. We felt as if we had stepped into a science fiction movie set in a far-away galaxy.

'Oh my god,' yelled Leo as he struggled to get his jacket on, hopping about on one foot while kicking his other foot into a down bootie.

I grabbed my camera gear and ran across the snow away from the tents to get photos and film with the guys and our camp in the foreground. I yelled back, 'Stand together and point towards it,' and clicked away madly on the camera. We were all on a high after that, just buzzing.

Then at 10pm, just as we'd climbed into our sleeping bags, the wind came up. Not wanting to miss the chance, we packed up camp and kited through the night, covering over 100km.

That signalled a change in the wind and we made it across the area we called No Man's Land, because no one had ever been through it before. It was not on the way to anywhere important, and being flat and featureless had not attracted any explorers before. We joined up to what could be described as the 'trade route' because it was where the majority of skiers travelled from the coast to the South Pole. By then our days were going well.

One of my goals was to cover 200km in a single day. Early on in the trip we never even got close. But after crossing No Man's Land we started flying and clocked up 185km, and the 200 was in easy reach. I was kiting along and as I glanced left, I saw Leo high above his pulk, the 8m rope between him and the pulk was tight. He was flying forward at heart-stopping speed. His arms were swinging wildly backwards – as if he was winding down the car windows (when windows had a manual handle). I was sure it was going to end badly.

He landed hard in an explosion of gear. His skis flew off and he tumbled a few times before coming to a stop. Luckily the snow was soft, but the pulk was still travelling at 35 km/hr towards him. Then, just before it ran over him as he lay on the snow, it veered to the right and stopped next to him. I halted immediately to check on him. Much to my amazement he was absolutely fine. Jean came back and we decided to camp there for the night. If only I'd had a camera pointing at Leo. Sadly, he declined encouragement to do it again for the camera.

The next day we did cover 201km, and in fact we managed over 650km in that four-day stint of perfect wind and snow conditions. Remember we were still towing 150kg pulks! It was all about the condition of the surface. Sometimes the surface was wood-hard with wave-like snow formations about one metre high, carved by the wind over eons of time. Sometimes, about 5-10% of the trip, we had 20 to 30cm of light, soft powder snow and the surface was faceted with incredible cup-shaped crystals. A snow nerd like me loved those crystals, especially when they caught the light in a hypnotic reflection of the sun.

There were times when I'd have music playing on my headphones (Jack Johnson, Moby, Pink Floyd, Shapeshifter, St Germain, or more often just a random compilation of tracks), sunglasses on, jacket unzipped, wearing only glove liners with my leg zips open. It was warm like that as we were going downwind, which meant the relative wind on us was minimal. It was peacefully quiet and we felt light on our feet, looping the kites in big circles for hour after hour.

After 50 days in the field, we finally found ourselves in Horseshoe Valley with mountains all around us and smooth powder under our skis, moving silently at 35 to 40 km/hr. Horseshoe Valley is where ALE's Patriot Hills blue-ice runway was when I first climbed Mt Vinson for Adventure Consultants. I recognised the mountains.

The snow was perfect for a few hours, then the wind stopped only 30km or so from our finish line at Union Glacier. We set up camp, which was actually a good thing because Leo was seriously keen on me trying to film with the stabilising gimbal we'd carried since the first cache. However, I wasn't sure I could kite, ski and film all at the same time.

The footage I'd got while kiting along a firm surface was shaky, not ideal for a big movie screen. The gimbal ensured we got the epic smooth stable shots for the film. But to steer a kite (similar to steering a mountain bike), ski and film another kiter in close proximity with the heavy and clumsy gimbal all at the same time, while wearing thick gloves could be compared to rubbing your belly in a clockwise direction with your right hand, your head in an anticlockwise direction with your left hand and kicking a soccer ball in the air with one foot all at once. Oh, and put on big thick gloves and a ski boot.

The next morning Leo set up the camera/gimbal while I launched my kite. He started recording it then handed it to me. I then spent 30 minutes following Jean with his kite and pulk as he flew across the soft snow at high speed. I gave the camera to Leo but he looked at me in disbelief, he hadn't started recording! 'Shit,' he yelled.

We tried again and I actually enjoyed following Jean at high speed. I passed him, then he passed me, and we tried out all sorts of angles. I gave the camera back to Leo and he checked it. Yes, we had the shot.

Leo really made the film in ways like that. It was never a hassle to get out of the tent to be filmed. If I wanted to reshoot a scene he was always up for it. I still wish I had taken more shots of certain things – the rock climbing, the icefall, the sastrugi skiing. But it was a balance of surviving unhurt without frostbite while moving enough each day and finishing the expedition.

As Leo had prepaid the rescue bond, if ALE's season came to an end (which it did two weeks after we finished) they would fly out and pick us up no matter where we were. Since they had taken us to Antarctica, it was their responsibility not to leave us there for winter. So this did add pressure on us to finish unsupported to save Leo's USD100,000 deposit.

We stashed the camera gear and headed off with high hopes for the buffet at Union Glacier that night. We kited up to a high col, ejected our kites in strengthening winds and skied below Union Glacier. 5km from camp, we clipped our pulks to our harnesses, put on touring skins and started the hour walk.

The walk into camp allowed us time to chat and reflect on what we'd achieved. We'd ignored the usual Antarctic targets such as the South Pole or Vinson Massif. People will always get more notoriety for going there faster, lighter, with fewer limbs etc. But we'd set a new standard, a new style not yet seen in that part of the world. Our objective was to climb a little-known mountain, not the biggest, or the hardest, just a spectacular technical peak. Quite possibly the most isolated mountain on Earth.

We'd figured out a modern and futuristic approach method using kites to power our journey, allowing us to carry back-breaking loads at high speeds for immense distances. I have no doubt more adventurers will travel this way in the future, opening up a new and exciting age of Antarctic exploration. I was proud to be a part of it and despite a fair bit of suffering, I loved every minute of it.

We arrived at Union Glacier just in time for the buffet dinner that we'd been dreaming about for weeks. We munched happily on salad, fresh vegetables and fruit, and as we ate we felt the first tugs of normal life reasserting themselves, with very different pulls to those of our now-worn harnesses.

No, it hadn't been easy. But we'd finished in good spirits and in good shape. Most importantly, we'd finished as good friends. On many expeditions team members fall out and never speak again after the trip. Leo and I are like brothers from a different mother, the same as only a few of my other friends. Jean and I are good friends, but not as close. I think I held him back on many occasions, but I'm fine with that. I'd like to think I helped them both as much as they helped me.

I added more fresh food such as meat and vegetables to the menu from my experience on other expeditions. It freezes into a block of ice, but most people don't realise you can just cook it from frozen. My mountaineering experience and guiding on easy terrain helped on many occasions. And hopefully my relaxed style.

We rested at Union Glacier for four days because we'd just missed a flight home. But that was okay. We enjoyed the extra time in Antarctica. We knew that as soon as we returned to South America we'd all vanish in our own directions. And we did. We all missed our families – Jean and Leo had two young children each. We were all happy to depart Punta Arenas for home.

Nine months later, thanks to the Banff Mountain Film Festival flying us all to Canada, we met up again for a few days together. It was very special. I loved it. We spoke at the Festival to around 1400 people. Leo was the true professional speaker, but Jean and I did okay. We thrilled the crowd with our stories – Leo almost getting dragged into crevasses, Jean getting a frostbitten scalp, the distance we travelled, the cold, the suffering, the comradeship we'd obviously had. We received a standing ovation.

I've given a slide show on the Spectre trip many times since and afterwards I always marvel at how differently people look at me after the talk. The classic comment is, 'I thought you were normal until seeing that'. Or they might say, 'What were you thinking?' Or maybe it is just a shaking of the head, a knowing smile and a look of respect. They love the story and are completely blown away by the images, the film and the tales of the adventure. A life highlight for sure.

23

NOW AND INTO THE FUTURE

I live in one of the world's most beautiful places, Lake Hawea. A busy day is when you see someone else on the beach and you walk past them and you look them in the eye and say, 'Hi' or just smile. I leave my keys in my car with my wallet in the car door. We hardly ever lock our house. We trust each other even if we don't know each other.

I've been enjoying more and more adventures close to home. Skiing, hiking or paragliding mountains I can see from my house. When you look at a landscape for years, I just love the feeling of looking back from it towards home. Then when you arrive home, that landscape doesn't look the same any more. You know more about it. You look at things differently and you often look beyond, or more carefully at part of it, the part you want to explore next.

I managed a first ski descent of Terrace Peak in 2018 – I can see it when I'm lying in my bed. We left home that day and met with the farmer early to ask for permission to cross his land, then headed up a ridge through the bush. It soon thinned out and we reached the snow, climbing around 1300m to the summit at 4pm. The face we wanted to ski was west facing and the snow had softened up during the afternoon sunshine. We skied fantastic smooth snow right off the summit down to the snow line 800m below where we unfolded our sleeping mats and bags and spent an awesome night sleeping under the stars.

The next morning we reclimbed to the summit and skied to the south, then walked through the bush and back to our cars. I still look back at that peak every afternoon when the sun is shining on it, and I remember that day.

Am I a brave person? Or crazy? Define crazy! If crazy means a love of adventure and trying something where the outcome is unknown, then yes. But I think of someone passing another car on a blind corner as crazy, or going fishing off rocks without a life jacket, drinking excessively, taking harmful drugs, going to protests when there is a pandemic, becoming obesely overweight. I think of these things as crazy. It's rolling the dice for an unknown outcome, or intentionally harming yourself. I'm afraid of dying, but I am even more afraid of not living!

I think of my risks as calculated. I've done the equivalent of crawling before I could walk, walking before I could run. I built up my skills slowly and got better and better at a skill very few on the planet can do well. I do admit that a fair amount of luck kept me alive when I was younger. But even now, in my 50s, I don't want to give up skiing, paragliding, kitesurfing or adventures.

Every chapter in the second part of this book has contained the possibility of losing my life. But I wouldn't give up the memories and experiences for anything. Once you live through something, if you have healed I don't think you wish to have not done it. You've moved on and are enjoying the other side. I've felt like through my life and all my mistakes, I've lived and done more than many would in several lifetimes.

As I get older I still love adventure, and I think back to my inspirational grandmother Dorothy. In her 90s her idea of adventure was to search the newspaper for a coupon, then cut it out and catch the bus across town to the store offering the deal, buy the shampoo or whatever was on sale, then bus home. This was her adventure. Everybody has their own adventures to live and now is the time. I've realised good health is a finite thing, never to be taken for granted. It is the most important thing in our lives and without it we can't help others or be there for family. It's through adventure that good health – both mental and physical – remains part of our lives. Get out there today and enjoy it . . .

I have a few sayings that I like to use, I guess you could call them Markisms

- It's easier to beg for forgiveness than to ask for permission.
- Worry is a wasted emotion.
- I want the last cheque that I write to bounce!
- 'What could possibly go wrong?' I stopped using this in 2014 after my helicopter crash. I enjoyed tempting fate on many occasions, such as abseiling off a massive rock face, or when I was about to ski a steep line. But I just can't do that any more, it feels wrong. Maybe it's an age thing. It's a good name for a book though!
- One of my favourite sayings and a great piece of philosophy is: 'Life's journey is not to arrive at the grave safely in a well-preserved body, but rather to skid in sideways, totally worn out, shouting, "Fuck! What a ride!" '

Mark Sedon